ANNA T. STONE

BOND TO CHAOS

INFERNAL TEMPTATIONS SERIES

BOOK I

Table of Contents

Content Warning

THIS BOOK CONTAINS themes and scenes that some readers may find sensitive or challenging. This story explores the complex relationship between a warlock and a succubus, touching on elements of dark fantasy and mature themes. Please be aware that this book contains but is not limited to:

- Sexual content and nudity
- Depictions of violence and blood
- Themes of temptation and corruption
- Intense emotional situations
- Occasional strong language

Reader discretion is advised. Please only read if you are comfortable with these themes.

Author's Note

DEAR READER,

Welcome to a tale where magic sparks and desires ignite.

In these pages, you'll meet a young warlock desperate to prove himself, and a seductress with secrets of her own. Their unexpected bond will challenge everything they thought, they knew about themselves.

As you follow their journey, you'll discover that the most potent magic often lies in the space between two hearts. This story is one of attraction, tension, and chaos. It asks: What happens when the very being you should resist becomes the one you can't live without?

I hope this story captivates you, challenges you, and perhaps even enchants you.

And when you turn the final page, caught in the afterglow of this story, I have one small request: If you enjoy this book, please consider leaving a review. Your words have the power to bring this tale to other readers, and for that, I'd be grateful.

Happy reading,

Anna

playlist

- Make You Mine - Madison Beer
- Monsters - All Time Low
- Streets - Doja Cat
- Only One Of The Girls - The Weekend, JENNIE, Lily-Rose Depp
- Dandelions - Ruth B
- Somewhere Only We Know - Keane
- If You're Meant To Come Back - Justin Jesso
- Fire Meet Gasoline - Sia
- Shameless - Camila Cabello
- Fire On Fire - Sam Smith
- Check Yes Juliet - We The Kings
- Team - Lorde
- You Belong With Me - Taylor Swift
- Fall For You - Second Serenade
- Misery Business - Paramore
- I Write Sins Not Tragedies - Panic at the Disco
- Gives You Hell - All-American Rejects
- Believer - Imagine Dragons
- Nobody - OneRepublic
- Enemy - Imagine Dragons & JID
- Apologize - Timbaland ft. OneRepublic
- Only Love Can Hurt Like This - Paloma Faith
- Running After You - Matthew Mole
- Dynasty - Miia
- Feels Like Tonight - Daughtery
- 11 Minutes - YUNGBLUD, Halsey, ft. Travis Barker
- Bones - Imagine Dragons

Old Letter

(from eight months ago)

Arcane Affairs Council

Rune City, Capital of the Lancaster Realms

Dear Aaron Kelley,

By decree of the High Council of Arcane Affairs, you are hereby exiled from Rune City and all affiliated magical institutions, effective immediately.

Your transgressions include practicing forbidden magic, endangering others through unauthorized experiments, and violating the Arcane Codex. In light of your family's service, exile is chosen over harsher punishment.

You are stripped of all Academy privileges and must depart Rune City by dawn. Return or further practice of forbidden magic will result in imprisonment.

This exile stands until the Council deems you reformed and no longer a threat.

May this time of solitude grant you the wisdom and restraint you so clearly lack.

E. Pendragon

Archmage Etherya Pendragon
High Council of Arcane Affairs

Chapter 1: The Ritual Gone Awry

AARON

The candles flickered ominously in the dim chamber, their dancing flames casting long, twisted shadows across the cold stone walls. I stood in the center of an intricate magical circle, my dark robes rustling softly as I prepared for the most ambitious ritual of my life.

This wasn't just any summoning ritual. This was my chance to prove to my family that exiling me to this godforsaken tower was a grave mistake. I would show them the true extent of my power. Demonstrate that my unconventional methods weren't just the rebellious actions of a wayward son but the mark of a genuinely gifted warlock.

The ritual chamber that I also use as my study was a circular room occupying the entirety of the tower's top floor and was a testament to months of meticulous preparation. Runes of power, meticulously carved into the floor and walls, pulsed with an eerie, yellow glow. The air seemed charged with the weight of the magic I was about to unleash. Ancient tomes and fragile scrolls littered the room's edges, their pages filled with forbidden knowledge that had taken me countless sleepless nights to decipher. The musty smell of old parchment mingled with the sharp, acrid scent of rare herbs and the metallic tang of blood used in the ritual preparations.

I took a deep breath, trying to center myself. The cool air filled my lungs, carrying the complex aroma of magic. This scent always reminded me of ozone and autumn leaves. I smoothed down my robes, a nervous habit I'd never entirely managed to shake. I stepped carefully into the center of the ritual circle. The moment my feet crossed the boundary, I felt it. The air crackled with latent energy, making the hair on the back of my neck stand on end. This was it. No turning back now.

I closed my eyes for a moment, visualizing the complex patterns of the spell in my mind. With one final steadying breath, I began the incantation.

The words of power rolled off my tongue, each syllable precise and carefully enunciated. My voice, low and steady at first, grew in volume and intensity as I felt the magic building around me. The ancient language felt foreign yet familiar on my lips, each word sending ripples through the air.

As the spell progressed, the candles' flames stretched and danced wildly, casting frenzied shadows across the walls. The runes carved into the stone began to glow brighter, their light pulsing in rhythm with the cadence of my chant.

A thrill of excitement coursed through me as I felt the spell taking hold. It was working! I could sense the barrier between worlds thinning, bending to my will. The air in the chamber grew thick and heavy, pressing against my skin like an invisible weight.

My confidence surged with each passing moment. I had spent years studying the darkest, most forbidden corners of magic, enduring the scorn and, eventually, the exile imposed by my family. But now, I would prove them all wrong. I would summon a being of immense power, bind it to my will, and demonstrate my skill to everyone.

The magic swirled around me, a tempest of raw power that I alone controlled. I felt invincible, unstoppable. At that moment, I truly believed I could reshape the world to my liking.

Just as I reached the climax of the spell, my voice rising to a near-shout as I prepared to tear open the veil between worlds, a movement caught the corner of my eye. My heart nearly stopped.

The stray cat—the same mangy creature I'd been feeding scraps to for weeks, had somehow slipped into the room. Its yellow eyes gleamed in the candlelight, reflecting the pulsing energy filling the chamber. It padded towards the ritual circle, drawn by the mystical forces it could surely sense.

"No!" I hissed, trying to shoo it away without breaking the incantation. Panic rose in my chest as I realized the danger. If the cat disrupted the circle, the consequences could be catastrophic.

But it was too late.

The cat's paw brushed against one of the carefully placed components, scattering a line of crushed herbs. The effect was instantaneous and devastating.

No longer perfectly contained, the magical energies exploded into a chaotic vortex. I was thrown backward, my back slamming against the cold stone wall with enough force to drive the air from my lungs. The wind howled through the chamber, a disorder born of wild magic, extinguishing the candles and sending papers flying in all directions.

Disoriented and gasping for breath, I struggled to my feet. My ears rang, and my vision swam as I tried to understand what had happened. Smoke filled the room, thick and acrid, stinging my eyes and burning my throat.

"By all the dark powers," I choked out, my voice barely above a whisper. "What have you done?"

As I blinked away tears, trying to peer through the smoky haze, a sinking feeling of dread settled in the pit of my stomach. I had lost control of the spell—the one thing a warlock should never do. Whatever I had summoned, it certainly wasn't what I had intended.

The smoke cleared, drifting in lazy spirals toward the high ceiling. I squinted, trying to make out shapes in the gloom. My heart pounded in my chest wildly.

Then I saw her.

Where the center of my ritual circle had been, a figure stood amidst the settling dust and dissipating magical energies. She was petite, shorter than me by at least a head, yet somehow imposing in a way that defied her small stature. Her skin glistened in what looked like a purple-ish hue, and curves that seemed to defy nature were barely contained by wisps of shadow that clung to her form like a second skin.

Long, flowing black hair shimmered with hints of deep purple, framing a face of otherworldly beauty. High cheekbones, full lips curved in a bemused smirk, and eyes—oh, those eyes. Glowing amber orbs with vertical pupils, like those of a cat, fixed on me with an intensity that made me feel like prey caught in the gaze of a predator.

But it was the bat-like wings folded against her back that truly drove home the reality of what I'd done. A slender, pointed tail ending in a heart-shaped tip swayed gently behind her, completing the picture.

I had summoned a succubus.

For a long moment, we stared at each other in silence. The only sound in the chamber was the soft patter of falling debris and the pounding of my own heart. I opened my mouth, but no words came out. What could I possibly say?

Then she spoke, her voice a melodic purr, sending shivers down my spine and weakening my knees.

"Well, well," the succubus said, a wicked smile on her lips. "What an... interesting predicament we find ourselves in, little warlock."

My mind raced, thoughts tumbling over each other in a frantic jumble. This wasn't what I had planned at all. I had to regain control of the situation and assert my power as the summoner. But as I looked into those hypnotic eyes, I realized with a sinking feeling that I might be in way over my head.

"I... I am Aaron Kelley," I managed to stammer out, trying to inject some authority into my voice. "Warlock of the Kelley bloodline. I have summoned you to this realm, and by the ancient laws of magic, you are bound to my will."

The succubus threw her head back and laughed, a sound like tinkling bells that was at once beautiful and terrifying. "Oh, my dear boy," she purred, stepping towards me. "I don't think you quite understand the situation you've created."

I swallowed hard, fighting the urge to step back as she approached. The air around her seemed to shimmer, and I could feel waves of power radiating from her form. It was intoxicating, a heady mixture of fear and desire that threatened to overwhelm my senses.

"I am Lizbeth," she continued, her eyes never leaving mine. "I have walked this earth and others for millennia. I've served in the courts of demon lords and brought empires to their knees with a whisper." She paused, now close enough that I could feel the heat radiating from her body. "And you, little warlock, have made quite the mess of things. It is obvious I am not what you intended to summon."

I bristled at her condescending tone, my pride momentarily overriding my fear. "I am no mere apprentice," I shot back. "I've mastered magics that would make lesser men tremble. This tower is my domain, and you will respect—"

My words were cut short as Lizbeth raised a delicate hand, pressing a single finger to my lips. The touch sent a jolt through my body, a mixture of icy fear and burning desire that left me speechless.

"Shh," she whispered, her face now inches from mine. "Let's not say things we'll regret, shall we? Your spell may have pulled me from my realm, but make no mistake—you are not my master."

Her wings unfurled, stretching to their full span as if to emphasize her point. They were magnificent, easily eight feet from tip to tip, blocking out what little light remained in the chamber. I felt very small at that moment, acutely aware of how outmatched I was.

The cat—the cause of all this chaos—chose that moment to emerge from its hiding place. It padded across the debris-strewn floor, meowing softly as it rubbed against

Lizbeth's leg. To my amazement, the succubus's expression softened as she looked down at the feline.

"Well, hello there, little one," she cooed, bending down to scratch behind the cat's ears. "Aren't you a clever thing? Slipping past all those wards and protections."

I watched in disbelief as the cat purred contentedly, entirely at ease in the presence of this otherworldly being. It was surreal, this moment of gentleness amidst the chaos of the failed ritual.

"Now then," Lizbeth said, straightening up and fixing her gaze on me again. "What exactly did you hope to accomplish with this little summoning of yours, Aaron Kelley?"

The way she said my name sent another shiver down my spine. I took a deep breath, trying to gather my thoughts. "I... I sought to prove myself," I admitted, the words tumbling out before I could stop them. "My family exiled me to this tower, believing my methods were too dangerous and unconventional. I wanted to show them the true extent of my power."

Lizbeth's expression was unreadable as she regarded me. "And instead, you've bound yourself to a force beyond your comprehension," she mused. "How deliciously ironic."

"Bound myself?" I echoed, a cold dread settling in the pit of my stomach. "What do you mean?"

The succubus smiled, but it didn't reach her eyes. "Your spell may not have gone as planned, little warlock, but it didn't fail entirely. We are connected now, you and I. Bound by magic, neither of us fully understand."

I felt the blood drain from my face as the implications of her words sank in. This was worse than I could have imagined.

Not only had I failed to assert dominance over the being I'd summoned, but I'd somehow tied myself to her in the process.

"What... what does this mean?" I asked, hating how small and uncertain my voice sounded.

Lizbeth's tail swayed lazily behind her as she considered the question. "It means, my dear Aaron, that we're stuck with each other for the time being. I cannot return to my realm, and you..." She paused, a wicked glint in her eye. "Well, let's just say your life is about to become far more interesting."

As if to punctuate her statement, a pulse of energy rippled through the room. The remaining candles sputtered to life, casting a warm glow over the disaster that was my ritual chamber. Books lay scattered across the floor, their pages fluttering in a nonexistent breeze. The once-pristine ritual circle was nothing more than a smudged mess of chalk and herbs.

I looked around, taking in the full extent of the chaos I had wrought. My carefully laid plans, my dreams of proving myself to my family—all of it had quite literally gone up in smoke. And now, I was bound to a being of immense power and questionable motives.

"What in the nine hells have I gotten myself into?" I muttered, more to myself than to Lizbeth.

The succubus laughed again, a sound that was becoming alluring to me. "Oh, Aaron," she said, reaching out to brush a stray lock of hair from my face. Her touch was electric, sending jolts of sensation through my body. "I think we're going to have so much fun together."

As I stood there, caught between fear and fascination, I couldn't help but wonder what the coming days would bring. I had sought power and recognition; instead, I had invited chaos into my carefully ordered world.

The cat, seemingly oblivious to the tension in the room, curled up at Lizbeth's feet and began to purr contentedly. It was such a mundane sound, so at odds with the supernatural events that had just transpired, I almost laughed.

Instead, I squared my shoulders and met Lizbeth's gaze. If this was to be my new reality, I would face it head-on. I was still a warlock of the Kelley bloodline, after all. I had faced challenges before, and I would face this one too.

"Very well," I said, injecting as much confidence into my voice as I could muster. "If we're to be... bound, then we should establish some ground rules."

Lizbeth's eyebrows raised, a look of amused surprise crossing her face. "Ground rules? My, my, you are a bold one, aren't you?" She stepped closer, her presence overwhelming my senses. "And what sort of rules did you have in mind, little warlock?"

As I opened my mouth to respond, I realized I was stepping into uncharted territory. None of the texts I had studied or the spells I had mastered had prepared me for this. I was about to negotiate terms with a being older than civilization itself, a creature of desire and chaos.

Chapter 2: An Unexpected Guest

AARON

I cleared my throat, ignoring how my pulse quickened as Lizbeth's gaze bore into me.

"First," I said, forcing my voice to remain steady, "this tower is my sanctuary. You will respect my privacy and my belongings." As I spoke, I gestured around the room, taking in the scattered books, the intricate magical instruments, and the various oddities I'd collected over the years. Each item represented hours of study, pushing the boundaries of what was considered 'acceptable' magic. They were more than mere possessions; they were the building blocks of my identity as a warlock.

A smirk played across Lizbeth's lips.

"Oh? And what makes you think I have any interest in your mortal trinkets, little warlock?" Her voice was a purr, low and melodious, with an edge that hinted at centuries of cunning and power.

I bristled at her condescending tone, feeling a flash of anger cut through my fear. Who was she to dismiss my life's work so casually? But I pressed on, determined to establish some semblance of control over the situation. "Second," I continued, my voice gaining strength, "no harming or seducing any visitors or residents of the nearby village. I may be exiled, but I won't have you wreaking havoc on innocent people."

The words sounded noble, even to my ears, but I couldn't help but wonder if they were more for my benefit than anyone else's. After all, wasn't I the one most at risk of falling under her seductive influence?

Lizbeth's laughter rang out. It echoed off the chamber's stone walls, seeming to fill every corner with its otherworldly melody.

"How noble of you," she said, stepping closer. The scent of exotic flowers wafted around her, an intoxicating mixture that made my head spin. "And tell me, Aaron Kelley, what do I get in return for following your... rules?"

The way she said my name made my breath catch in my throat. It was as if she had woven a spell with those two simple words, imbuing them with a power that resonated through my very being. I swallowed hard, acutely aware of her proximity. Her eyes, with their vertical pupils, reminded me of a cat toying with its prey. And in that moment, I knew without a doubt that I was the mouse in this scenario.

"I can offer you knowledge," I said, gesturing to the books scattered around the room. "My library contains rare texts on magic and the occult. Surely there's something there that would interest a being of your... caliber."

As I spoke, I moved towards one of the bookshelves that had somehow remained standing during the chaos of the summoning. My fingers trailed along the spines of ancient tomes, their titles written in languages long dead to the mortal world. These books were my pride and joy, each one a hard-won trophy in my quest for knowledge.

"This one," I said, pulling out a heavy volume bound in what looked suspiciously like boars' skin, "contains rituals that were old when the pyramids were young. And this," I added, indicating a slender manuscript with silver-edged pages, "is said to hold the secrets of binding starlight itself."

Lizbeth's eyes lit up at that with a predatory gleam. She moved closer, her wings rustling softly as she examined the books. "Knowledge, you say? Now that is an intriguing offer." She ran a finger along the spine of the manuscript, her touch almost reverent. I couldn't help but notice the sharp, claw-like nail that glinted in the candlelight. "Very well, little warlock. I'll play by your rules... for now."

I let out a breath I hadn't realized I'd been holding. It wasn't much, but it was a start. A foundation, however shaky, upon which we could build some sort of coexistence. "Good," I said, trying to regain some semblance of control. "Now, about our... connection. How exactly does it work? And more importantly, how do we break it?"

The question had been burning in my mind since the moment I realized the extent of what I'd done. The texts I'd studied had spoken of the dangers of improperly conducted summonings, of the bonds that could form between summoner and summoned. But none had prepared me for this.

Lizbeth's expression turned serious for the first time since her arrival. "It's not that simple, I'm afraid," she said, her voice losing some of its seductive edge. "The magic that binds us is ancient and complex. Breaking it could have... unforeseen consequences."

"Consequences?... What kind of consequences?" I asked, though a part of me feared the answer.

She shrugged, a maddeningly casual gesture given the gravity of the situation. Her wings flexed slightly with the movement, drawing my attention to their leathery expanse. "Death, madness, the unraveling of reality itself. Who knows? Magic of this magnitude is unpredictable."

I ran a hand through my hair, frustration mounting. This was not how I had envisioned my grand ritual ending.

In my mind, I had seen myself standing triumphant, a powerful entity bound to my will, ready to do my bidding. Instead, I found myself bound to a being whose power I could scarcely comprehend, with no clear way to undo what I'd done.

"So we're stuck like this? For how long?" The words came out more plaintive than I'd intended, betraying the fear and uncertainty that churned within me.

"Until we find a way to safely sever the connection," Lizbeth said, her tail swaying lazily behind her. The heart-shaped tip flicked back and forth, hypnotic in its rhythm. "Which means, my dear Aaron, that you and I are going to be spending a lot of time together."

The implications of her words hit me. I had summoned a succubus—a being of desire and chaos—and now I was bound to her indefinitely. My carefully ordered life, my plans for redemption in the eyes of my family, all of it had been thrown into disarray in the span of a single night.

Images flashed through my mind. My father's disappointed scowl, my brother's mocking laughter, the whispers that had followed me through the halls of the magic academy. I had come to this tower to prove them all wrong, to show that my unconventional methods weren't just the act of a rebellious mage. And now...

"I need to sit down," I muttered, stumbling over to a nearby chair and collapsing into it. The ornate wooden seat, carved with protective runes and sigils, had been my throne of sorts. From here, I had conducted countless experiments, pored over forbidden texts, and dreamed of the day I would prove my family wrong. Now, it felt more like a refuge, a place to hide from the reality of what I'd done.

Lizbeth watched me with a mixture of amusement and something that might have been sympathy. It was hard to tell with her; every expression seemed to hold layers of meaning, centuries of experience shaping even the simplest gesture. "Come now, it's not all bad," she said, perching on the arm of the chair. Her proximity sent a surge through me, a blend of fear and... something more. Something I wasn't entirely ready to think about too deeply.

"Think of the possibilities, Aaron," she continued, her voice taking on a silky quality that seemed to bypass my ears and go straight to my core. "With my knowledge and your power, we could accomplish great things."

I looked up at her, suddenly wary.

In that moment, I was acutely aware of the stories I'd read about demons and their bargains, of the way they could twist words and intentions to their own ends. "What kind of 'great things' did you have in mind?"

Her smile was both dazzling and dangerous, a combination that made my heart race. "Oh, I have so many ideas," she purred, leaning in closer. I could feel the heat radiating off her body and smell the intoxicating scent that clung to her skin. "We could delve into magics long forgotten by your kind. Unlock secrets that would make the greatest wizards of your age weep with envy. Or perhaps," she added, her voice dropping to a whisper, "you'd like to show your family just how powerful you've become?"

The offer was tempting. I couldn't deny that. The thought of returning to the capital, Lizbeth at my side, demonstrating powers beyond anything my family could dream of... it was intoxicating. But I knew better than to agree to anything so quickly, especially with a being like her.

"But first," Lizbeth said, pulling back slightly, "I think we should focus on making this tower a bit more... comfortable for my extended stay."

As if on cue, the stray cat—the unwitting catalyst for this entire situation—jumped into my lap, purring. I absently stroked its fur, my mind reeling from the events of the night. The familiar sensation helped ground me, reminding me of simpler times when my biggest concern was making sure the little creature was fed.

"I suppose we'll need to find you a room," I said, the absurdity of the situation finally hitting me. I was discussing living arrangements with a demon as if she were nothing more than an unexpected houseguest. A hysterical laugh bubbled up in my throat, but I swallowed it down. Losing my composure now would not help matters.

Lizbeth's eyes sparkled with mischief. "Oh, I'm sure we can come to some arrangement that's... mutually beneficial."

The implication in her words was unmistakable. I felt my face flush, a warmth spreading through me that had nothing to do with the lingering energies of the ritual. "That's not—I didn't mean—" I stammered, trying to regain my footing in the conversation.

She laughed again, the sound somehow mocking. It filled the chamber, seeming to dance on the air itself. "Relax, little warlock. I'm only teasing... for now."

The 'for now' hung in the air between us... I stood up abruptly, dislodging the cat from my lap. It let out a disgruntled meow before sauntering off to find a more stable resting place. "Right. Well, it's late, and I'm exhausted. We can discuss the details of our... arrangement in the morning."

Lizbeth rose gracefully, her wings folding neatly against her back. The movement was fluid, almost hypnotic, and I found myself staring despite my best efforts not to. "As you wish," she said, her voice a low purr that seemed to caress my senses. "I'll just make myself at home, shall I?"

Before I could protest, she sauntered out of the room, her hips swaying in a surely intentional way. Watching her go, the torchlight played off her curves, casting entrancing shadows with each step she took.

As she disappeared from view, I let out a long, shaky breath. The full weight of the night's events came crashing down upon me, and I felt my knees go weak. I leaned against the chair for support, my mind racing with the implications of what had transpired.

As I began to clean up the mess from the failed ritual, my mind raced with questions. How would I explain Lizbeth's presence and more pressingly, how long could I resist the temptation that Lizbeth represented? She was a being of desire incarnate, created to seduce and corrupt. And I... I was only human despite my magical abilities. The connection between us thrummed like a living thing, a constant reminder of her presence.

The stray cat meowed softly, rubbing against my leg as I worked. I looked down at it, shaking my head. "You've really done it this time, haven't you?" I muttered. The cat, of course, offered no response beyond another contented purr. Its simple presence was oddly comforting.

Setting books back on shelves and sweeping up the remnants of shattered artifacts, I couldn't help but reflect on the path that had led me here. My exile, my desperate quest for more power and knowledge—it all seemed so foolish now, in light of what I'd done. And yet, a small part of me was thrilled by the possibilities that Lizbeth represented. With her by my side, could I achieve everything I'd ever dreamed of and more?

It was well past midnight by the time I finished restoring some semblance of order to the room. My body ached, a bone-deep weariness that was more than just physical exertion. The magical energies I'd channeled during the ritual had taken their toll, leaving me drained in a way I'd never experienced before.

As I made my way through the winding corridors of the tower towards my bedchamber, I could hear Lizbeth moving about in one of the spare rooms. The sound of her footsteps, lighter than they should be for a being of her size, was punctuated by the occasional rustle of her wings. And underlying it all was a tune—a haunting melody that she hummed as she explored her new surroundings.

I paused outside my door, listening to the otherworldly song. It was beautiful in a way that defied description, with notes that seemed to exist between the standard tones I was familiar with. The melody spoke of ancient forests and starlit skies, of passions both exquisite and terrible. It called to something deep within me, awakening feelings and desires I hadn't even known existed.

Coming back to my senses. I realized I had been standing there for several minutes, swaying slightly to the rhythm of Lizbeth's song. I shook my head, trying to clear the fog that had settled over my thoughts. This, I realized, was just a taste of the power she held—the ability to enthrall with nothing more than a simple tune.

I entered my room and collapsed onto the bed, not even bothering to remove my robes. The familiar scent of old books and candle wax surrounded me, a comforting reminder of my life before this night. But now, underlying it all was a new scent— exotic flowers, the unmistakable mark of Lizbeth's presence in my tower.

As exhaustion overtook me, my last coherent thought was a silent prayer to whatever dark powers might be listening: Please don't let me regret this more than I already do.

Chapter 3: Pleasant Surprises

LIZBETH

Swaying my hips most seductively, I sauntered out of the room, my tail swishing behind me with each step. I decided to make myself at home and explore my new environment, curious about what secrets this mortal's abode might hold. This tower, I discovered, had quite a few rooms, more than I'd initially expected. The rooms, though, were dusty and neglected; had no one lived with this warlock? It was almost pitiful. I wrinkled my nose in disgust as I ran a finger along a grimy surface. Eventually, I made my way to what seemed like a library, the scent of old parchment and leather-bound tomes tickling my nostrils. Perhaps there was something of value here after all.

"Well, well," I murmured, viewing the collection of books. "What treasures have you been hoarding, little warlock?"

I plucked a book from its resting place. It was a grimoire, its cover adorned with symbols that would drive most mortals mad. But to me, they whispered secrets of power and chaos.

As I leafed through the pages, my amusement grew. This Aaron Kelley was no ordinary summoner. The margins were filled with notes in a cramped, eager hand—observations and theories that spoke of a mind both brilliant and dangerously ambitious.

"You're full of surprises, aren't you?" I chuckled, replacing the book.

My fingers trailed over various magical instruments, each thrumming with latent power. A crystal ball that showed glimpses of other realms, a dagger whose edge seemed to cut the very air—toys, really, compared to the artifacts I'd seen in the demon lords' vaults. And yet, there was something endearing about the collection. It spoke of a hunger for knowledge, a desire to push boundaries.

As I strolled through the room, taking in every detail, my thoughts inevitably drifted to the peculiar event that had brought me to this mortal plane. The jarring sensation of being forcibly pulled from the infernal realm still lingered. And then... there was Aaron. The image of him standing there, wide-eyed and clearly panicked, was etched into my memory.

Yet beneath that initial fear, I had sensed an undercurrent of raw, untamed power that had taken me by surprise. It was... intriguing, to say the least. When I answered the summons, I definitely did not expect someone like him. He was a far cry from the usual lot who dared to call upon beings of my caliber—no lecherous old mage or desperate, sniveling mortal seeking favors beyond their means.

No, this Aaron was different. People like him, with that spark of genuine potential, don't usually summon my kind. We're typically called upon by the weak, the corrupt, or the truly wicked. But this? This was something else entirely. It was glaringly obvious that he had stumbled into this situation purely by chance, a novice playing with forces far beyond his comprehension. The thought brought a smirk to my lips. How delightfully unpredictable.

I paused before a large mirror, its surface rippling like quicksilver. My reflection stared back at me, but my eyes were drawn to a new addition—a small, intricate crest etched into the skin on my chest. Aaron's magical signature, binding us together.

"Now, isn't that interesting," I mused, tracing the mark with my fingernail.

In all my millennia of existence, traversing countless realms and encountering innumerable magical phenomena, I'd never encountered a binding quite like this. It wasn't the crude, domineering magic most summoners used—the kind that sought to chain and subjugate through brute force. No, this was something far more subtle and potentially far more powerful. The intricacy of the design spoke of a depth of magical knowledge that belied Aaron's apparent youth and inexperience. I couldn't help but wonder if he truly understood what he had done or if this was yet another example of his raw talent manifesting in ways he couldn't possibly fathom.

I closed my eyes, feeling the connection between us. Images flashed through my mind—memories, but not my own. A young boy struggling to control his burgeoning magical abilities. A stern-faced man—his father?—was looking on with disappointment. Years of study, of pushing beyond accepted limits. And always, always, that burning desire to prove himself.

My eyes snapped open, a slow smile spreading across my face. "Oh, Aaron," I purred. "What have you gotten yourself into?" My wings twitched with restless energy. I needed to know more.

I sauntered back to one of the rooms I had decided to claim as my sleeping quarters, selecting the one closest to Aaron's. As I pushed open the heavy wooden door, I couldn't help my distaste. The room was functional but utterly lacking in style or comfort.

"This place desperately needs a feminine touch." I cast my gaze around the sparse chamber, already envisioning the changes I'd make. Plush fabrics, rich colors, perhaps a few strategically placed candles to create the right ambiance... But those were idle fantasies for now. "I suppose I'll have to make do for the time being," I sighed, my tail twitching with irritation.

I moved to the windows, peering out at the world beyond. The village Aaron had mentioned lay nestled in the valley below, a cluster of thatched roofs and winding streets. Even from this distance, I could sense the life force of its inhabitants—a tempting buffet of desires and fears.

A smirk tugged at my lips as I recalled Aaron's "rule" about not harming or seducing the villagers. So noble, so *human* of him. As if a few words could truly bind a being like me.

And yet... I found myself oddly reluctant to disregard his wishes entirely. There was potential here, in this tower, and in Aaron himself. Potential that could be far more satisfying than a few quick thrills in the village.

As I stared idly at my view below, a soft melody escaped my lips. It was a song I'd picked up from my travels throughout time. It spoke of freedom, of roaming through a forest beneath starlit skies. The lyrics whispered of a life filled with passion and desire, of the thrill of the hunt and the sweet release that followed. My sultry and seductive voice filled the cold stone tower. The song was a reminder of who I truly was—a succubus, a creature of darkness and sin.

I moved around the room as I sang my song, thinking back to a time when I used to walk among mortals more freely. I remembered their rituals, their ways of showing care and building connections. And suddenly, I knew exactly what I needed to do. I needed to gain his trust. To make him see me as more than just a demon to be controlled or feared.

As the first rays of dawn began to creep through the window. I made my way to the chamber Aaron had summoned me in last night. I stepped onto a small balcony just in time to see the sun crest the horizon.

The sight took my breath away. There was no actual sunlight in the infernal realms—only the eternal glow of hellfire. But this... this was something else entirely. The world was bathed in warm, golden light, transforming the drab countryside into a fusion of color and life.

For a moment, I stood there, basking in the simple beauty of it all. How long had it been since I'd allowed myself to appreciate such things? There was little room for simple pleasures in the endless power struggles of the demon courts.

With a flutter of my wings, I descended to the tower's lower levels, seeking out the kitchen. The room was small and cluttered, a far cry from the grand feasting halls of the infernal palaces. But it would serve my purpose.

I began to explore the space, and my heightened senses quickly identified the freshest ingredients. Eggs from the henhouse, bread baked just yesterday, herbs hanging from the rafters—all the makings of a proper mortal breakfast.

As I set about preparing the meal, I couldn't help but chuckle at the absurdity of it all. Here I was, a being of immense power and age, reduced to playing housemaid for a young warlock. And yet, there was a certain thrill to it. I, Lizbeth, ancient succubus and newly minted chef, would enjoy every moment of this new game.

"Let the games begin, little warlock. Let's see just how far our bond can take us."

Chapter 4:
Aftermath and
Realizations

AARON

I woke up with sunlight streaming through the narrow window of my bedchamber. My dreams last night were vivid and disjointed, filled with fire and shadow. I saw myself standing atop the tower, Lizbeth by my side, power crackling at my fingertips. I saw my family cowering before me, their faces terrified, and through it all, I heard the sound of Lizbeth's laughter.

For a moment, I lay there, trying to convince myself that the events of the last night had been nothing more than a particularly vivid dream. But the lingering scent of flowers and the faint sound of humming from elsewhere in the tower quickly dispelled that notion.

With a groan, I sat up, running a hand through my messy hair. "What have I gotten myself into?" I muttered, staring at my reflection in the small mirror hanging on the wall. The face that stared back at me looked haggard, with dark circles under the eyes and a pallor that spoke of magical exhaustion.

I stood up, my muscles protesting the movement. The ritual had taken more out of me than I'd realized. My mind raced with plans and contingencies as I changed into fresh robes. I needed to establish some sort of routine, some semblance of normalcy in this new, chaotic reality.

Taking a deep breath, I steeled myself for the encounter that awaited me. I couldn't hide in my room forever, tempting as the thought might be. With one final glance in the mirror, I pushed open the door and stepped into the corridor.

The scent of something cooking wafted through the air, a surprising smell given the circumstances. Curious and more than a little wary, I followed my nose to the small kitchen area I rarely used. The sight that greeted me stopped me in my tracks.

Lizbeth stood at the stove, her back to me, wings folded neatly against her back. She was humming that haunting tune again, her hips swaying slightly to the rhythm as she tended to something in a pan. The domesticity of the scene was so at odds with her demonic nature that, for a moment, I could only stare.

"Are you going to stand there all day, or would you like some breakfast?" Lizbeth asked without turning around. Her voice had an amused lilt that made me wonder if she'd been aware of my presence the entire time.

I cleared my throat, trying to regain my composure. "I... didn't know demons needed to eat," I said, immediately regretting the words as soon as they left my mouth. Smooth, Aaron. Very smooth.

Lizbeth turned then, a playful smirk on her lips. "We don't, strictly speaking," she said, gesturing with a spatula. "But after a few millennia, you learn to appreciate the finer things in life."

"Besides," she added, her eyes glinting mischievously, "I thought you might need to keep up your strength. We have a lot to discuss, after all."

I felt my face flush at her implication, but I forced myself to move further into the kitchen, where I sat at a table I hardly ever used. "Right. Of course." I paused, sniffing the air. "Is that... bacon?"

"Indeed it is," Lizbeth said, returning her attention to the stove. "I hope you don't mind, but I took the liberty of exploring your pantry. You really should stock up more often, you know. A growing warlock needs his nutrients."

The normalcy of the conversation was almost more disturbing than if she'd been ranting about the souls of the damned. I sat at the small table, watching Lizbeth expertly flip the bacon. "Where did you learn to cook?" I asked, genuinely curious.

She shrugged a fluid motion that made her wings rustle softly. "Here and there. You'd be surprised how often culinary skills come in handy when trying to tempt mortals." She glanced over her shoulder, winking at me. "The way to a man's soul is often through his stomach, after all."

I swallowed hard, unsure how to respond to that. Thankfully, I was saved from having to formulate a reply by the arrival of the stray cat. It strolled into the kitchen, tail held high, and made a beeline for Lizbeth.

To my surprise, Lizbeth's face softened as she looked down at the feline. "Well, hello there, little one," she cooed, reaching down to scratch behind its ears. The cat purred loudly, rubbing against her legs. "I suppose you'd like some breakfast too, hmm?"

As I watched Lizbeth interact with the cat, a thought struck me. "It doesn't seem afraid of you at all," I mused aloud.

Lizbeth glanced up at me, an eyebrow raised. "Animals often see things more clearly than humans do," she said cryptically. "They respond to energy, to intention. Perhaps this little one knows I mean it no harm."

I pondered her words as she finished cooking, setting a plate of bacon and eggs in front of me before taking a seat across the table. The cat, given its own small saucer of milk, curled up contentedly at Lizbeth's feet.

I took a bite of the food—which was, I had to admit, delicious—and I couldn't help but marvel at the surreality of the situation. Here I was, having breakfast with a succubus in my tower kitchen as if it were the most natural thing in the world.

"So," Lizbeth said, leaning back in her chair, "shall we discuss the terms of our... arrangement?"

I set down my fork, meeting her gaze. Her eyes, with their vertical pupils, were as mesmerizing as ever, but I forced myself to focus. "Yes, I suppose we should," I said, trying to inject some authority into my voice. "As I said last night, this tower is my sanctuary. I need to be able to continue my work without... interference."

Lizbeth nodded, her expression unreadable. "Of course. I have no interest in disrupting your studies. I might even be able to assist you in some areas. I've picked up quite a bit of knowledge over the millennia, you know."

I had to admit the offer was tempting. The wealth of knowledge Lizbeth must possess was enough to make any scholar of the occult salivate. But I knew I had to be cautious. "And what would you want in return for this assistance?"

Lizbeth's smile widened, showing just a hint of fang. "Oh, nothing too onerous. Perhaps the occasional outing to the village? I promise I'll be on my best behavior," she added, seeing my expression. "No seducing or corrupting the locals. I simply miss the hustle and bustle of mortal life sometimes."

I considered her request. It seemed reasonable enough, and keeping Lizbeth cooped up in the tower indefinitely didn't seem wise. "Alright," I said slowly. "But you'll need to... disguise yourself somehow. I can't have the villagers seeing a demon walking among them."

"Of course," Lizbeth said, waving a hand dismissively. As I watched, her appearance shimmered and changed. Her wings receded and her tail disappeared entirely. In moments, she looked for all the world like a stunningly beautiful human woman. "Will this suffice?" Lizbeth uttered.

I blinked, taken aback by the transformation. "That's... impressive," I admitted. "But how do I know you won't use this ability to cause mischief when I'm not around?"

Lizbeth's expression turned serious. "You have my word, Aaron Kelley," she said, "I swear by the ancient laws that bind our kind that I will not use my powers to harm or unduly influence the mortals of this realm without your express permission."

The weight of her oath hung in the air between us. I could feel the magic in her words, a binding as real and tangible as any spell I'd ever cast. "I... thank you," I said, somewhat awkwardly. "I accept your oath."

Lizbeth nodded, her form shimmering once more as she returned to her true appearance. "Now then," she said, her tone lightening, "shall we discuss the more... personal aspects of our arrangement?"

I felt my face flush again, but I forced myself to meet her gaze. "What did you have in mind?"

She smiled. "Well, as a succubus, I do have certain... needs. Energy that must be replenished. But don't worry," she added, seeing my expression, "I won't drain you dry. In fact, seeing how you're back on your feet so quickly after summoning me, it seems there's more to you than the average mortal. A healing factor perhaps... this can be something mutually beneficial for the both of us."

I shifted uncomfortably in my seat, processing Lizbeth's words. Based on books I've read, I knew what a succubus 'needs' are, but I needed more time to devise a strategy. However, before I could formulate a response, a thought struck me.

"You know," I began, surprising myself with the words, "I think I owe you a bit of a reward for this breakfast. It's been... unexpectedly pleasant."

Lizbeth's eyebrows rose. "Oh? And what did you have in mind, dear warlock?"

I took a deep breath, hardly believing what I was about to suggest. "How about that outing to the village? We could go today if you'd like."

The succubus's face lit up with genuine excitement, her tail swishing behind her. "Really? You mean it?"

I nodded, a small smile tugging at my lips despite my better judgment. "Yes, but remember our agreement. You'll need to maintain your human disguise and no mischief."

"Of course, of course," Lizbeth said, waving a hand dismissively. In an instant, she shimmered and transformed back into her human guise. "Shall we depart now?"

I glanced down at my somewhat disheveled appearance. "Perhaps after I've had a chance to make myself a bit more presentable."

An hour later, we were going down the winding path from my tower to the nearby village. Lizbeth, in her human form, looked every bit the part of a visiting noblewoman in a simple yet elegant dress I'd conjured for her. I'd opted for a more subdued outfit, not wanting to draw too much attention. The one she had done herself was a little... much for the eyes.

Lizbeth's eyes darted everywhere as we walked, taking in the lush forest around us with childlike wonder. "It's been so long since I've seen a mortal realm like this," she mused. "Everything seems so... alive."

I found myself watching her more than our surroundings, fascinated by this softer side of the demon. "I suppose the infernal realms aren't known for their natural beauty," I remarked.

Lizbeth laughed. "Not unless you find lakes of fire and fields of tormented souls beautiful."

As we approached the village, I felt a twinge of anxiety. "Remember," I whispered, "we're just a pair of travelers passing through. Nothing unusual."

Lizbeth nodded, her expression becoming more neutral as we entered the village. The bustling market square was alive with activity, with villagers haggling over fresh produce and handcrafted goods.

To my surprise, Lizbeth handled herself admirably. She chatted with the local vendors, admired the craftsmanship of a blacksmith, and even cooed over a litter of puppies being sold by a farmer. Not once did she let her demonic nature slip through.

As the sun began to set, casting long shadows across the streets, we made our way back to the tower. Once inside, I let out a long breath and dropped the protection spell I'd been maintaining all day.

Lizbeth's eyes widened in surprise. "You... you had a cloaking spell on us the entire time?" she asked, a note of admiration in her voice.

I nodded, trying not to show how drained I felt. "Couldn't risk anyone sensing your true nature."

She studied me with newfound interest. "You're full of surprises, little warlock. The power and stamina required for such a feat... perhaps I've underestimated you."

Warmth bloomed in my chest at her words, though I tried to dismiss it. "Yes, well... I'm glad you enjoyed the outing."

Lizbeth's smile softened, becoming almost genuine. "I did. Thank you, Aaron. It's been a long time since I've experienced such simple pleasures."

As I prepared for bed, I couldn't shake the feeling that something had shifted between us. Lizbeth's gaze lingered on me as she retreated to her room.

Lying in my bed, staring at the ceiling, I tried to sort through the tumult of emotions coursing through me. What game was Lizbeth playing? And, more importantly, why did part of me want to play along?

Chapter 5: A Dance
of Sin and Desire

LIZBETH

I padded down the hallway, drawn to his door like a moth to a flame. Pausing outside, I listened to the rhythmic rise and fall of his breathing, savoring the moment as Aaron slept blissfully unaware of my presence.

In the darkness, my eyes glowed. The thrill of a delicious meal had my mouth salivating. It was fascinating how his vulnerability could stir such delight within me—a mere mortal oblivious to the chaotic dance at play.

What would he think if he knew the actual depth of my allure? I chuckled silently at the thought. This was not merely about conquest; it was about power, knowledge, and the intoxicating thrill that came from bending a will to my own.

I turned the doorknob, anticipation pulsing through me. Tonight, I would explore the boundaries of our unusual alliance and perhaps add a few twists of my own. I watched Aaron as he slept, his muscular chest rising and falling with each deep breath, his tousled jet-black hair framing his handsome face. I had been observing him for a day now, studying his every move. His guard has been up, but tonight,

I intend to go beyond the physical and into the realms of the carnal.

I gently climbed on top of him, straddling him. With a flick of my wrist and a murmured incantation, I cast a spell that allowed me to enter his dreams. It was night-time in the dream, and he was fast asleep under a tree. I walked over to him, waking him with a kiss on the cheek. His eyes flew open, and he gasped at the sight of me. I appeared before him, alluring and seductive, wearing a silk dress, my body glowing with a soft ethereal light. The dream world was a place of endless possibilities, a realm where the most exquisite and depraved desires could be brought to life, and I intended to take full advantage of that.

As I moved closer to him, my spectral wings fluttered softly, sending a gentle caress of cool air over his body. I could see the desire building in his eyes, a hunger that matched my own. I had been craving this moment, the chance to explore Aaron's most intimate desires and to have him explore mine in return.

I straddled his dream-self, feeling the weight of my body pressing against his own. I could feel the heat radiating from him, the energy that fueled his every action. I reached down and cupped his face in my hands, my thumbs brushing against his stubbled cheeks. "Tonight, we're going to explore a different kind of magic," I whispered into his ear.

I began with a slow, sensual kiss, savoring the taste of him, the way his lips yielded to mine. I could feel the warmth of his tongue as it danced and entwined with my own. I felt one of his hands move up to my waist, pulling me closer. With his other hand he trailed fingers down my spine.

The dream world responded to our desires, creating a sumptuous setting around us. It was filled with the scent of exotic flowers and spices, the air thick with a heady perfume that seemed to make our senses even more attuned to each other.

As we kissed, I felt Aaron's hands moving up, cupping my breasts, his thumbs teasing my nipples through the thin fabric of my dress. I let out a soft moan, my body responding to his touch, my energy building with every caress. I needed more. With a thought, I had his shirt gone.

I pulled away from the kiss, moving down to his neck, my tongue tracing a heated path along his pulse. I could feel the energy pumping through his veins, and I knew that I was driving him mad with desire. I moved further down, my lips and tongue exploring the planes of his chest, the taste of his skin intoxicating me.

I shifted my weight, moving down to kneel between his legs. I looked up at him, my eyes locked with his, as I slowly unbuttoned his pants. I could see the anticipation in his eyes, the pure, unadulterated need that he felt for me. I felt his erection spring free, and I took it in my hand, stroking it with a slow, deliberate motion.

Aaron's breath hitched, his body tensing as I took him in my mouth. I felt him shudder beneath me, his hands moving to tangle in my hair. His taste, sweet as I felt my power building with every stroke of my tongue, every taste of his essence.

I could feel the energy of the dream world swirling around us. I knew I was taking a risk, drawing on his energy through the dream world, but I couldn't resist. It was pure ecstasy. I moved to straddle Aaron, my body hovering over his. I reached down, needing more of everything. I began to line him up to guide him inside me, but then, all of a sudden, the dream shattered, and his hand clenched around my neck.

"What the hell are you doing!"

I felt Aaron's grip on my neck loosen, but his intense dark eyes remained fixed on me. "Start talking, demon. What the hell were you doing in my head?" he demanded. I couldn't help but let my eyes flash defiantly. "What I *must* do to survive, warlock. Or would you prefer I go mad with hunger?"

"Hunger?" His brow furrowed adorably. "Explain yourself. Now." I sighed dramatically, relishing the moment. "Very well. I require... certain interactions to sustain myself. I'll become ravenous without them, and neither of us wants that."

Aaron released me, shoving me aside and getting up from the bed. I almost missed his touch. "What kind of interactions?" he asked, his voice wary. "Physical contact, primarily," I said, smoothing my hair with practiced nonchalance. "It doesn't have to be... extensive. But I need something."

His expression hardened, and I had to admit, it was rather becoming on him. "And you thought coming onto me in my sleep was the best approach?"

"I was desperate!" I snapped, letting my frustration show. "I know you have been trying to avoid the nature of what I am."

Aaron paced the room. I couldn't help but admire the sight of him; for a mortal, he was quite good-looking.

"Fine. What exactly do you need to... not go crazy?"

I counted off on my fingers, enjoying his discomfort. "Touch, at the very least. A kiss would be better. More... intimate contact would be ideal, but—"

"Let's start small," Aaron interrupted, his cheeks flushing slightly. Oh, how delightful. "I'm not entirely opposed to helping you, but we need boundaries."

I raised an eyebrow, unable to resist teasing him. "Oh? Not as repulsed by me as you let on, are you?"

Aaron glared at me, but I could sense the uncertainty behind his bravado. "Don't push your luck, demon. I'm willing to help but on my terms."

"Very well," I said, letting a small smile play on my lips. "What do you propose?"

Aaron thought for a moment, and I savored his internal struggle. "We can start with...touch. But nothing more without explicit discussion and agreement. Understood?"

I nodded, feeling a mixture of relief and amusement. "Agreed. Though I warn you, little warlock, you may enjoy our arrangement more than you expect."

Aaron rolled his eyes, but I caught the hint of curiosity in them. "Don't count on it. If we're done here, get out of my room so I can get back to sleep."

As I got off the bed and started walking towards the door to leave, I couldn't resist glancing back at him, savoring the sight and licking my lips. This was going to be far more entertaining than I had initially thought.

Chapter 6:
Dangerous
Distraction

AARON

Getting enough sleep has been challenging ever since Lizbeth arrived two weeks ago. Unable to sleep after her feeding frenzy last night, I decided to busy myself. I stood in the center of my study, preparing for my most ambitious spell since the night I accidentally summoned Lizbeth.

This wasn't just any spell—this was my chance to prove that I could still push the boundaries of magic, even with the complication of my unwanted demonic houseguest. I've been trying to crack this spell for a while now.

I took a deep breath, trying to center myself. Smoothing my hands down my robes, I closed my eyes for a moment and visualized the complex patterns of the spell in my mind.

I began the chant, my voice resonating with power as the words flowed from my lips. The spell was taking hold, its tendrils of energy weaving through the air around me. I could feel the magic building, pulsing with each syllable I uttered. The energy in the room filled, crackling with potential. My heart raced with excitement. It was working! The fruits of my labor were finally manifesting, and I could sense the raw power at my fingertips, ready to be shaped by my will.

And then, just as I reached a crucial juncture in the spell, a voice cut through my concentration like a knife.

"My, my, little warlock. Aren't we looking serious today?"

I stumbled over the next word of the incantation, my rhythm broken. The magical energies swirled chaotically for a moment before settling back into a more stable pattern. I gritted my teeth, forcing myself to continue the chant while shooting a glare in the direction of the interruption.

Lizbeth lounged in the doorway, her lithe form silhouetted against the dim light of the hallway. A crimson gown clung to her curves, accentuating her figure and leaving little to the imagination. The gown's low-cut neckline revealed the ample swell of her breasts, while the split of the dress offered teasing glimpses of her shapely legs and her long, flowing black hair cascaded down her back, shimmering with a hint of deep purple.

Her expression was filled with mischief, and that infernal smirk played across her lips. She knew exactly what she was doing, and she was enjoying every moment of it. The sight of her stirred something deep within me, a primal desire that I couldn't quite shake. I knew better than to fall under her spell, but the temptation was almost overwhelming.

The magical energies swirling around me reacted to her presence, growing more turbulent and unpredictable. I struggled to maintain my focus, my chant wavering as I fought against the distraction she presented.

With a roll of her eyes, Lizbeth pushed off from the doorway and sauntered towards me, her hips swaying seductively with each step. I could feel her power washing over me, her charm working its insidious magic as she drew closer. I gritted my teeth and clenched my fists, determined not to give in to her allure.

"Oh, come now, little warlock," she purred, her voice dripping with honeyed venom. "Is it really so difficult for you to concentrate with me around? Or is it that you find me just a little too... distracting?"

I bit back a retort, focusing all my energy on the incantation. I could feel the magical energies fusing once more, responding to my will despite Lizbeth's attempts to derail me. With a huff, she spun on her heel and stalked across the room.

As I reached a crucial point in the spell, I heard a soft laugh from across the room. My eyes snapped open, and I saw Lizbeth lounging on a nearby chaise, her crimson gown pooled around her.

"Don't mind me, little warlock. I'm just enjoying the show."

I gritted my teeth and tried to ignore her, focusing on the intricate patterns of magic I was weaving. But her presence was like an itch I couldn't scratch, constantly pulling at the edges of my attention.

From the corner of my eye, I saw her stretch languidly, her movements slow and deliberate. The slit in her skirt revealed more than just a glimpse of leg, and I found my gaze drawn to her despite my best efforts.

"You know," she drawled, twirling a lock of her shimmering black hair around one finger, "I could teach you so much more than these dusty old books ever could."

I faltered for a moment, the words of the spell catching in my throat. Shaking my head, I redoubled my efforts, pouring more power into the incantation.

Lizbeth sighed dramatically, shifting on the chaise. "It's all so... boring, isn't it? All this studying and practicing. Wouldn't you rather do something more... exciting?"

I found myself wondering what she meant by 'exciting,' my mind conjuring images that had no place in spell casting.

"Focus," I muttered to myself, clenching my fists. The spell was nearing its climax, and I couldn't afford any more distractions.

But Lizbeth rose from the chaise, her movements fluid and graceful. She began walking towards me.

"You know, I've seen countless warlocks over the millennia. But you... you're different, Aaron. There's something special about you."

I tried to block out her words, but they wormed their way into my mind. Special? What did she mean by that? Was she just trying to manipulate me, or was there truth in her words?

The magical energies around me fluctuated, responding to my wavering concentration. I gritted my teeth, forcing myself to focus on the spell. But it was becoming increasingly difficult to ignore Lizbeth's presence.

She now stood directly behind me. I couldn't see her, but I could feel her breath against my ear.

"I could show you things," she whispered, her voice low and enticing. "Secrets of magic that no mortal has ever known. Power beyond your wildest dreams."

My hands trembled slightly as I continued the incantation, the words coming out less steady than before. The offer was tempting, more tempting than I cared to admit. But I knew better than to trust a demon, especially one as cunning as Lizbeth.

"All you have to do," she continued, her voice barely more than a breath, "Is ask."

The spell reached its crescendo, the magical energies swirling around me in a maelstrom of power. But my concentration was shattered, my mind torn between the spell and Lizbeth's tempting words.

The magic began to slip from my control, the carefully woven patterns unraveling. I felt a surge of panic as I realized I was losing my grip on the spell.

"Damnit!" I growled, struggling to regain control. But it was too late. The magic collapsed in on itself, dissipating in a flash of light and a rush of wind that sent papers flying across the room.

I stood there, panting, my robes disheveled and my hair wild. The failure stung, made all the worse by the knowledge that I had let Lizbeth get to me.

"Well," Lizbeth's voice cut through the haze, sounding far too amused for my liking. "That was certainly... entertaining."

"Get out!" I snarled.

Lizbeth raised an eyebrow, that infuriating smirk still firmly in place. "Now, now, is that any way to treat your houseguest? Especially one who's so... interested in your work."

I took a deep breath, trying to calm the anger that threatened to boil over. "This is not a game, Lizbeth. These spells are dangerous. Your presence here is... distracting, to say the least."

"Distracting?" She practically purred the word, taking a step closer. "Why, Aaron, I had no idea I had such an effect on you."

I felt my face flush, "That's not what I meant, and you know it. If you're going to stay here, you need to respect my work. These experiments are important."

Lizbeth's expression softened slightly, a hint of genuine curiosity creeping into her eyes. "Very well," she said, her voice losing some of its teasing edge. "Perhaps we could come to an arrangement. I'll behave myself during your little magical endeavors if you explain what you're trying to accomplish."

I hesitated, weighing my options. On the one hand, sharing my research with a demon seemed like a monumentally bad idea. On the other, if it meant I could work without constant interruptions...

"Fine," I said, letting out a resigned sigh. "But you have to promise to remain silent during the actual casting. No comments, no questions, no... distractions. Understood?"

Lizbeth's smile was dazzling, and for a moment, I forgot to breathe.

"Oh, Aaron, I do so love it when you try to set rules for me. Very well, I accept your terms."

I swallowed hard, suddenly acutely aware of how close she was standing. I took a step away from her, trying to put some distance between us.

"Right," I said, my voice sounding strained. "Well, let's get this place cleaned up, and then I'll walk you through the basics of what I'm trying to accomplish."

As we worked to restore order to the space, I couldn't help but steal glances at Lizbeth. She glided with elegance, each movement smooth and intentional. Even the simple task of gathering the disordered papers seemed like a dance when she did it.

Once the room was back in some semblance of order, I retrieved my grimoire from my desk. As I flipped through the pages, checking for any damage, Lizbeth peered over my shoulder.

"Fascinating," she murmured, her breath tickling my ear. I tried to ignore the way my pulse quickened at her proximity. "These symbols... they're not like any mortal magic I've seen before."

I cleared my throat, focusing on the text before me. "That's because they're not entirely mortal in origin."

Lizbeth's eyes lit up with genuine interest. "And what were you trying to accomplish with your little spell earlier?"

I hesitated for a moment, then decided that honesty was the best policy. After all, if we were going to be stuck together for the foreseeable future, a bit of trust might go a long way.

"I'm creating a spell to amplify my abilities," I admitted. "To push beyond the limits of what's considered possible."

Lizbeth's eyebrows rose, a look of respect crossing her features. "Ambitious," she said, her voice tinged with admiration. "And potentially very dangerous. No wonder you were so upset by my interruption."

I nodded, feeling a small surge of pride at her words. "Exactly. These spells require intense concentration and precision. The slightest mistake could have catastrophic consequences."

"I see," Lizbeth said, her tone thoughtful. "Well then, shall we try again? I promise to be on my best behavior this time."

I eyed her warily, searching for any sign of deceit. But all I saw was genuine curiosity and... maybe a hint of excitement?

I realized that Lizbeth might actually be interested in my work, beyond just using it as an opportunity to tease me.

"Alright," I said, making my decision. "But remember, absolute silence during the casting. If you have questions, save them for after."

Lizbeth mimed, zipping her lips. I rolled my eyes at her antics but couldn't help the small smile that tugged at the corners of my mouth.

As I prepared to start this process over once more. I found myself hyper-aware of Lizbeth's presence. She had settled into a corner of the room, and I noticed she had taken her human form as if to adhere to my rules. She sat on a chair, her eyes following my every move, intense and unblinking.

I took a deep breath, centering myself. The familiar tingle of magic moved across my skin. The words of the incantation flowed from my lips, smooth and sure, the magic swirling into a vortex of energy.

I could see Lizbeth leaning forward, her expression rapt with fascination. But true to her word, she remained silent, not disturbing the charged atmosphere.

As I reached the climax of the spell, I felt something shift. The magic surged, stronger than I had ever felt it before. It was as if a dam had broken, releasing a flood of power that threatened to overwhelm me.

For a moment, panic gripped me. This was more than I had anticipated, more than I was sure I could control. But then, just as I felt my grip on the spell beginning to slip, I felt… something else.

A warmth spread through me, starting from the center of my chest and radiating outward. It was unlike anything I had experienced before—not the raw, chaotic energy of my own magic, but something different.

Startled, I realized what it was—Lizbeth. Her vast and ancient power was intertwining with my own, steadying me and amplifying the spell in ways I had never imagined possible.

The final words of the incantation left my lips, carried on a wave of power that made the very air shimmer. For a heartbeat, nothing happened. Then, with a sound like reality itself tearing, a portal opened right in front of me.

Chapter 7: New Realms

AARON

It was beautiful and terrifying all at once. Swirling energies of every color imaginable danced within its depths, and through them, I caught tantalizing glimpses of other realms. Worlds beyond my wildest imagination flashed before my eyes, each stranger and more wondrous than the last.

"By all the dark powers," I breathed, staring in awe at what we had created.

Lizbeth was at my side instantly, her eyes wide with wonder. "Aaron," she whispered, her voice filled with a reverence I had never heard from her before. "Do you realize what you've done?"

I shook my head, still struggling to process the magnitude of what had just occurred. "I... I didn't intend for this to happen. The spell was supposed to enhance my magical abilities, not open a gateway to other realms."

Lizbeth laughed, a sound of pure joy that seemed to resonate with the energies swirling before us. "Oh, my dear warlock, I do love these 'accidents' of yours," she said, facing me. "Don't you see? This is so much more than a simple spell. You've tapped into something mystical that bridges the gap between mortal magic and the powers that shape reality itself."

As I stared into her glowing amber eyes, I felt a surge of... something. Pride? Excitement? Or perhaps something deeper, more dangerous. The space separating us appeared to sizzle with a force unrelated to the dimensional rift and entirely linked to our mutual bond.

Lizbeth reached out, her hand hovering just above the portal's surface. "May I?" she asked, her voice barely above a whisper.

I nodded, unable to form words. As her fingers brushed against the swirling energies, the portal pulsed, sending out a wave of power that made my skin tingle. Lizbeth gasped, her eyes closing in what looked like ecstasy.

"It's... incredible," she breathed, her voice filled with wonder. "I can feel the essence of a thousand worlds, all connected, all pulsing with life and magic."

Caught up in her excitement, I reached out to touch the portal myself. The moment my fingers made contact, I felt a jolt of energy, unlike anything I had ever experienced. It was as if I could sense the very fabric of reality, the threads that bound all of existence together.

And then, without warning, the portal began to fluctuate wildly. The energies swirled faster and faster, colors bleeding into one another in a dizzying kaleidoscope. I felt a pull as if the portal was trying to draw me in.

"Lizbeth!" I cried out, panic rising in my chest. "We need to close it!"

She nodded, her expression suddenly serious. Without hesitation, she grabbed my hand, intertwining her fingers with mine. The contact sent a shock through my system, but I pushed the sensation aside, focusing on the task.

We began to chant together, our voices rising in unison as we wove a spell of containment and dismissal. The words came to me instinctively, as if I had known them all my life. Lizbeth's voice blended with mine, creating harmonies that seemed to resonate with the very foundations of reality.

Slowly, painfully, the portal began to shrink. The wild energies calmed, settling into a more stable pattern. We pushed with a final surge of power, and the gateway snapped closed with an audible pop.

The sudden silence was deafening. I stood there, panting, my hand still clasped tightly in Lizbeth's.

"Well," Lizbeth said after a moment, her voice slightly breathless. "That was... invigorating."

I couldn't help it. I laughed. It started as a small chuckle and quickly grew into full-blown, slightly hysterical laughter. After a moment, Lizbeth joined in, her melodious giggles blending with my deeper sounds.

As our laughter subsided, I became acutely aware that we were still holding hands. Lizbeth seemed to realize it at the exact moment. Our eyes met, and for a heartbeat, neither of us moved.

Then, gradually, with apparent hesitation, our hands parted. The absence of her touch left me feeling peculiarly unsettled, as though a vital part of myself had vanished.

Shaking off the lingering sensation, I turned my focus inward. I started jotting down observations in my grimoire regarding techniques for creating a gateway. The pages filled with my hurried scrawl, capturing not just the mechanics of the magic but also attempting to make sense of the chaos that had just unfolded.

"So," Lizbeth said, breaking the awkward silence that had fallen between us. "It seems your little experiment was more successful than you anticipated."

I nodded, still trying to process everything that had happened. "Successful, yes, but also incredibly dangerous. We could have been pulled into that portal or, worse, released something from another realm into ours."

Lizbeth's eyes sparkled with excitement. "But think of the possibilities, Aaron! The power we just wielded was beyond anything I've experienced in centuries. And the way our energies intertwined..." She trailed off, a look of wonder on her face.

I couldn't deny the thrill that ran through me at her words. The magic we had performed together was unlike anything I had ever experienced. It was intoxicating, addictive even. But the rational part of my mind screamed caution.

"We need to be careful," I said, running a hand through my hair. "This kind of power... it's not meant for mortals. Or even demons, for that matter. We could easily lose control."

Lizbeth stepped closer, her eyes locked on mine. "But that's what makes it so exciting, isn't it? The danger, the unpredictability. Tell me you didn't feel more alive in that moment than you ever have before."

I swallowed hard. "I... I can't deny that it was exhilarating," I admitted. "But we can't just rush into this blindly. We need to study what happened and understand the forces we're dealing with."

A slow smile spread across Lizbeth's face. "Now you're talking my language, little warlock. Research, experimentation... I do so love a scholarly approach to chaos."

I felt a small smile tugging at the corners of my mouth. "I thought you'd be more interested in the destructive potential of what we just did."

Lizbeth laughed. "Oh, Aaron. There's so much you still don't know about me. I may be a demon, but I'm also thousands of years old. You don't live that long without developing an appreciation for knowledge."

I considered her words, realizing that there was indeed much about Lizbeth that I didn't understand. Perhaps it was time to change that.

"Alright," I said, making a decision. "If we're going to continue these experiments, we need to work together. No more distractions or attempts to undermine each other. Deal?"

Lizbeth's eyes widened in surprise, then softened with something that might have been respect. "Deal," she said, holding out her hand.

I hesitated for a moment before taking it. The moment our skin made contact, I felt the familiar spark of energy pass between us. It wasn't the overwhelming surge of power from before but a gentler current, a reminder of our shared connection.

As we shook hands, I couldn't help but wonder what I was getting myself into. Working closely with a demon, especially one as unpredictable as Lizbeth, was dangerous in more ways than one.

I glanced around the room, noticing the scattered components and the lingering traces of magical energy. We began to clean up for the second time today, and I thought to myself that I might need to cast a barrier around my things if this magic was going to be this unpredictable.

Watching Lizbeth helping out again, it occurred to me that perhaps she had been as bored and frustrated as I had been, trapped in this tower with no real outlet for her powers.

"You know, I never thought I'd say this, but I'm glad you're here, Lizbeth. What we just did... I don't think it would have been possible without you."

Lizbeth paused in her task of reorganizing my books, a look of genuine surprise crossing her features. "Why, Aaron," she said, her voice softer than I'd ever heard it, "I do believe that's the nicest thing you've ever said to me."

I felt my face heat up and quickly turned back to the bookshelf. "Yes, well... don't let it go to your head. We still have a lot of work to do, and I'm sure you'll find plenty of ways to annoy me in the process."

Her laughter filled the chamber, and I found myself smiling. As we continued to work, she asked me various questions about magical artifacts that I had and books she had been reading in my library. She may not have been what I initially wanted, but I sometimes didn't mind having her around.

Chapter 8: The Exchange

LIZBETH

I lounged on the windowsill of Aaron's study as I watched the young warlock pore over his grimoire, a little black book he seems to always keep within his cloak, chained to his belt. The afternoon sun cast a warm glow over the room, illuminating the dust motes that floated in the air.

As I watched Aaron's movements, a frown creased my brow. Something about this mortal puzzled me, a conundrum I couldn't quite unravel. How could he not see it?

The raw magical energy that radiated from Aaron was unlike anything I had encountered in centuries. Yet, the warlock seemed oblivious to the true extent of his abilities.

He's strong, I admitted to myself, far more potent than he realizes. With the right...

The thought trailed off, and I felt a slow smile spread across my face. In my realm, strength was everything. It determined one's place in the infernal hierarchy, dictated who ruled and who served. And here was this mortal, with power that could rival some of the lesser demon lords, fumbling through spells like a novice.

He's rough around the edges, certainly, I thought, my gaze softening slightly as I watched him mutter a curse and furiously scratch out a line in his notes. But with more guidance, he could be... magnificent.

The term caught me off guard, and I hastily dismissed it from my mind. I was a demon, after all. Magnificence shouldn't matter to me, only power and how to use it.

As Aaron's latest experiment filled the room with a shimmering, violet light, my mind wandered to the incredible feat we had accomplished together. The portal we had opened, however briefly, had been a thing of terrible beauty. I could still feel the echoes of that power thrumming through my veins.

Once we perfected that magic, I realized with a jolt that I could return home...

The thought should have filled me with joy, but instead, it left me feeling strangely hollow. The possibilities this magic presented was endless.

Why stop at simply going home?

A plan took root in my mind, dark and tempting. With that kind of power, I could reshape reality itself, carve out my own realm, and become a power to rival the greatest of demon lords.

Lost in my scheming, I almost missed the frustrated sigh that escaped Aaron's lips. I blinked, refocusing on the present moment, and decided it was time to sate my curiosity.

"Tell me, little warlock," I purred, stretching languidly before sauntering over to his desk. "Are there others like you in this world? Other mortals who wield such... intriguing magic?"

Aaron looked up, his dark eyes momentarily clouded with confusion before focusing on me. He ran a hand through his disheveled hair, leaving it standing up at odd angles.

"Others like me?" he repeated, a hint of bitterness creeping into his voice. "I'm... not sure, to be honest. The magic I practice isn't seen as 'true' magic in this world."

I raised an eyebrow, genuinely intrigued. "Oh? Do tell."

Aaron pushed his chair back from the desk, his frustration evident in the set of his shoulders. "The magic counsel, the so-called 'guardians' of arcane knowledge, they frown upon what I do. They call it dangerous, rebellious." He let out a humorless laugh. "They call us radicals."

"Us?" I prompted, leaning against the desk and fixing Aaron with my intense gaze.

"There are whispers," Aaron admitted, his voice dropping low as if he feared being overheard. "Rumors of others who practice the old ways, who seek to push the boundaries of what's possible. But we're scattered, isolated. The council makes sure of that."

My mind raced with the implications—a whole network of untapped potential, of mortals with power they didn't fully understand or appreciate. The possibilities were intoxicating.

"And what do you think of these others?" I asked, keeping my tone casual. "These fellow 'radicals'?"

Aaron's eyes lit up with a fire that made my breath catch in my throat. "I think they're the future," he said, his voice filled with passion. "Magic isn't meant to be contained, regulated by some stuffy old men who are too afraid to see what it could become. We're on the cusp of something revolutionary, Lizbeth. I can feel it."

As I looked at him, his face alight with determination and his aura pulsing with untamed power, I felt something shift within me. My plans of using this magic for my own gain suddenly seemed... smaller, somehow.

Perhaps, a treacherous voice whispered in the back of my mind, there's more to be gained by nurturing this potential than by stealing it for myself.

The thought was dangerous, utterly at odds with everything I had ever known. And yet, as I watched Aaron return to his grimoire with renewed vigor, I couldn't quite shake the feeling that I stepped into something far greater than I had initially imagined.

Oh, little warlock, I thought, a mixture of amusement and something dangerously close to affection coloring my internal voice, you have no idea what you've awakened, do you?

With a small shake of my head, I moved to Aaron's side, peering over his shoulder at the complex diagrams and incantations scrawled across the pages.

"Well then," I said, allowing a hint of excitement to creep into my voice, "shall we see just how radical we can be?"

Aaron looked up at me with surprise and nodded, a slow smile spreading across his face.

"Let's," he agreed.

The sun had disappeared from the sky. We had been at this for hours, the young warlock eagerly sharing his knowledge of this world's magical structures while I helped him decipher the ancient languages that enhanced his spellcasting. The exchange of knowledge was surprisingly enjoyable.

"So, what kinds of magic is there in this realm?" I asked, tracing a finger along a diagram in one of Aaron's dusty tomes.

Aaron nodded, his eyes bright with enthusiasm. "Traditionally we have Elemental magic, Alchemy and there is also original magic. Magic that occurs in a bloodline allowing its user to create new possibilities but that's a story for another time." He said looking away as if a memory floated by. "But my research suggests these categories are rather limiting."

I smirked, remembering the fluid, chaotic nature of infernal magic. "Oh, little warlock, you have no idea how right you are."

He leaned forward, intrigued. "What do you mean?"

"In my realm, magic isn't confined to neat little boxes," I explained, enjoying the way his eyes widened at my words. "It's wild, unpredictable. It's about will and intent more than rigid structures."

Aaron's brow furrowed as he considered this. "That sounds... dangerous."

I couldn't help but laugh. "Oh, it is. Deliciously so."

We turned our attention back to the ancient text before us, a crumbling scroll covered in symbols that seemed to shift in the fading light.

"This passage here," I said, pointing to a particularly complex glyph, "it's not just a spell component. It's a key to unlocking a deeper understanding of the magical frequencies around us."

Aaron's eyes lit up with excitement. "Really? How can you tell?"

I tapped the side of my head, grinning. "Millennia of experience, darling. Now, let me show you how to properly channel that energy..."

As I guided Aaron through the correct pronunciation and gestures, I felt that familiar tingle of magical energy building in the air. It was intoxicating, this blending of our knowledge and power.

But now I wasn't thirsting for knowledge. It had been a long day, and I was feeling for something else... something more delectable. I licked my lips and moved to where Aaron sat in his chair.

Despite our agreement on light touches, we had quickly graduated to more filling methods. He understood that I needed physical intimacy for sustenance. And at this moment, I was running low. My energy was ebbing, and I required a refill. Aaron, being my sole source of sustenance, knew what that entailed. The hunger radiating off me was palpable.

"Aaron," I whispered, letting a husky undertone linger in his name. I could see the effect my voice had on him.

I moved closer, my body a whisper away from his. In a swift yet soft movement, I straddled his lap, my hands resting against his chest. I could feel his hardness straining against his trousers, his closeness intoxicating.

"I need this, Aaron," I whispered, leaning in close. As my breath caressed his ear, I felt him shudder, "And we agreed, remember?"

I leaned in, brushing my mouth against his. The kiss was slow and deliberate. My tongue teased his, tasting and exploring with a reverence that made his heart race.

I began to explore his body, my hands roaming his chest, my lips following the trail of my touch. I could feel the electricity coursing through him.

As I explored him, I reveled in the shivers I sent down his spine. Every part of him called out for me, and I knew he wanted to feel me, every inch of me, underneath his hands.

Finally, I pulled away, leaving Aaron panting for breath. I glanced down at him, feeling his heart pounding as he waited for what would happen next.

In this game we played, the desire was intoxicating, but the need was even greater. I needed him, and in our agreement, I would only take what he was willing to give. The power in that knowledge was aphrodisiac in itself.

I watched as he leaned back, letting the chair absorb his weight, his body taut with anticipation. His chest rose and fell rapidly, his breaths fast and shallow. He was ready, willing to let me take what I needed.

With a nod, I leaned in, my hands skipping down his body and coming to rest on his thigh. My lips were a hair's breadth away from his ear, "Just close your eyes, Aaron," I whispered, my fingers trailing a path up his thigh.

As Aaron's eyes fluttered closed, I let my fingers move along the bulging fabric of his trousers. I explored him through the fabric, each stroke driving him mad with arousal. I could hear the low groans he tried to stifle, but it was futile.

Then, I slipped my hand inside his trousers, wrapping my fingers around the hardened flesh of his length. Aaron couldn't hold back the gasp that tore itself from his lips, pleasure radiating from where I touched him.

As my hand moved along his erection, Aaron's hips bucked, chasing the sensation. He was beyond the point of no return, his release was imminent. His breath caught in his throat as I squeezed gently, and with a final, choked gasp, Aaron came.

Flowing down his staff, I licked from his stem to the tip, sucking what energy remained inside. He let out another gasp, failing to contain it. I looked up at him, ensuring he felt my gaze as I bore my fangs with a gentle smile, not piercing his skin, just adding to the thrill. I cleaned him up, kissing and licking everything away, savoring the energy I've now gained.

Pulling away my hand. I could sense how much he wanted to pull me back, to take my mouth and force my lips back onto his crotch.

I leaned back, my eyes filled with a hunger that was still unsatisfied. But we both knew that we had reached the limit of our agreement. This was as far as we would go tonight.

I rose from his lap, my body glowing with renewed energy. The sight of him watching me, his heart still pounding, brought me a sense of satisfaction that had nothing to do with the energy I had just absorbed.

Chapter 9: Just Two People

AARON

On my way to the study, I found Lizbeth sitting on the edge of my desk, leafing through one of my old spell books.

"Morning," I mumbled, moving towards the small side table where I kept my tea-making supplies.

Lizbeth looked up. "Good morning, little warlock. Slept well?"

I grunted noncommittally, focusing on preparing my tea. The silence stretched between us, and the smell of lavender and lemon filled the air as I began making my tea.

Finally, Lizbeth snapped the book shut. "You know what? We need a change of scenery. Let's go to the market today."

I blinked, caught off guard. "The market? Why?"

"Because," she said, sliding off the desk with slender grace, "you've been cooped up in this tower for far too long. A little fresh air and human interaction will do you good."

I opened my mouth to protest, but Lizbeth cut me off. "No arguments. We're going. Besides, I want to try some of that food you're always going on about."

Before I knew it, we were walking down the winding path to the village, Lizbeth practically bouncing with excitement.

She'd transformed into her human guise, and sometimes this form still took me off-guard. She looked very much the same, only no fangs or tail and her skin was slightly tanned. She looked beautiful in both forms.

The market was a riot of color and noise. Vendors called out their wares, children darted between stalls, and the scent of spices and food filled the air. I felt overwhelmed almost immediately, but Lizbeth seemed to enjoy the scenery.

"Oh, look at that!" she exclaimed, dragging me towards a stall piled high with spiky fruits. "What are those?"

"Dragon fruit," I muttered, trying to avoid eye contact with the grinning vendor. "They're not actually from dragons."

Lizbeth laughed, a sound that turned heads. "Pity. That would have been interesting. Oh! What's that smell?"

She pulled me through the crowd, following her nose to a food stall where a grizzled old man was frying something in a large wok. The smell was indeed intoxicating, a mix of spices and sizzling meat that made my mouth water despite myself.

"Two, please!" Lizbeth chirped, holding up two fingers.

The old man nodded, scooping generous portions of the steaming concoction into paper cones. Lizbeth handed one to me, her eyes shining with anticipation.

"What is it?" I asked, eyeing the unfamiliar food warily.

"No idea," Lizbeth grinned. "That's the fun part. Come on, try it!"

I looked at the cone in my hand and paid the old man. It was filled with some kind of fried meat and vegetables, liberally doused in a dark, sticky sauce. The smell was enticing, but I hesitated.

Lizbeth had no such reservations. She took a big bite, her eyes widening in pleasure. "Oh, by all the circles of hell, this is amazing!" she moaned, loud enough to draw curious glances from nearby shoppers.

Encouraged by her reaction, I took a tentative bite. The flavors exploded on my tongue—sweet, spicy, savory, all at once. It was like nothing I'd ever tasted before.

And it was hot. Very, very hot.

I coughed, my eyes watering as the spice hit the back of my throat. Lizbeth looked at me, concern mixing with amusement on her face.

"Are you okay, Aaron?" she asked, trying and failing to suppress a giggle.

I nodded, unable to speak. My mouth felt like it was on fire. I looked around frantically for something to drink, but there was nothing in sight.

Lizbeth, realizing my predicament, quickly grabbed a cup of ale from a nearby stall, tossing a coin to the startled vendor. She handed it to me, and I gulped it down gratefully.

"Not used to spicy food, are we?" she teased, patting me on the back as I continued to cough.

I glared at her, but there was no real heat in it. "How are you eating that so easily?" I wheezed.

She shrugged, taking another bite. "Demon, remember? We're used to things being a little... heated."

I groaned at the pun, which only made her laugh harder. By now, we'd drawn quite a crowd. The old man at the stall was beaming, clearly pleased that his food had made such an impression.

"Come on," Lizbeth said, linking her arm through mine. "Let's find you something a little more... suitable for your delicate palate."

As we moved through the market, I couldn't help but smile. Despite my embarrassment, there was something freeing about being here, away from the tower and my books. Lizbeth's enthusiasm was infectious, and I found myself relaxing, even enjoying the bustle and noise.

We stopped at several more food stalls, Lizbeth insisting on trying everything that caught her eye. She convinced me to try a sweet pastry filled with some kind of fruit preserve, which was mercifully free of spice. As we walked and ate, I realized that this was the most normal I'd felt in a while.

"See?" Lizbeth said, licking sugar off her fingers in a way that was decidedly un-ladylike. "Isn't this better than being cooped up in that musty old tower?"

I nodded, surprised to find that I meant it. "It is. Thank you for... for dragging me out here."

She smiled, a softer expression than her usual mischievous grin. "Anytime, little warlock. Anytime."

As we continued our exploration of the market, I found myself stealing glances at Lizbeth. She was in her element here, charming vendors and passersby alike with her quick wit and dazzling smile.

I watched as Lizbeth flitted from stall to stall, her excitement contagious. Despite my initial reluctance, I decided to let go and enjoy this moment. We sampled exotic fruits, haggled over trinkets, and even tried our hand at a game of ring toss.

"Look, Aaron!" Lizbeth called, holding up a gaudy necklace adorned with fake gems. "Isn't it hideous? I love it!"

I couldn't help but laugh. "It's certainly... something."

She grinned and draped it around her neck. "I think it brings out my eyes, don't you?"

"If by 'brings out' you mean 'completely clashes with,' then yes, absolutely," I teased.

Lizbeth gasped in mock offense. "How dare you! I'll have you know this is the height of de— fashion."

We burst into laughter. For a moment, we weren't a warlock and a succubus bound by a magical accident. We were just two people enjoying a day at the market.

As the sun began to set, casting a warm glow over the village, Lizbeth tugged on my sleeve. "One last stop," she insisted, pulling me towards a small booth tucked away in a corner.

An old woman sat behind a table covered in various crystals and charms. Her eyes twinkled as we approached.

"What can I do for you, dears?" she asked, her voice surprisingly strong for her apparent age.

I watched as Lizbeth inched closer with a mischievous look. "We're looking for something special. Something... magical."

I tensed, worried she might be pushing too far, but the old woman just smiled. "Aren't we all, dearie? Here, try this."

She handed Lizbeth a small, smooth stone. As soon as it touched Lizbeth's palm, it began to glow with a soft, pulsing light.

Lizbeth's eyes widened in genuine surprise. "It's warm," she whispered.

I leaned in, with hidden curiosity. The stone seemed to be responding to Lizbeth's energy, its glow intensifying as she turned it over in her hand.

"It likes you," the old woman chuckled. "Why don't you keep it? No charge."

As we walked back towards the tower, Lizbeth kept pulling out the stone, watching it glow in the gathering darkness. Her childlike wonder at such a simple thing was... endearing.

"Thank you," I said softly. "For today. It was... fun."

Lizbeth smiled a real smile without any of her usual mischiefs. "You're welcome, little warlock. Sometimes we all need a little fun."

I looked at Lizbeth as we walked back to the tower, the glowing stone still cradled in her hands. Her fascination with such a simple trinket sparked my curiosity. There was so much I didn't know about her despite our unusual living arrangement.

"Lizbeth," I began, my voice hesitant. "I was wondering... what was your life like before you ended up here?"

She glanced at me, surprise flickering across her features. "My, my, Aaron. Getting personal, are we?"

I shrugged, trying to appear nonchalant. "Just curious. You know so much about me, but I know very little about you."

Lizbeth was quiet for a moment, her fingers tracing the smooth surface of the stone. When she spoke, her voice was softer than usual. "It's been a long time since anyone asked me about my past."

We reached the tower, and I unlocked the door, gesturing for her to enter first. As we climbed the stairs, Lizbeth began to speak.

"I've existed for millennia, Aaron. I've seen empires rise and fall, watched as mortals discovered fire and invented the wheel." She paused, a faraway look in her eyes. "I've served in the courts of demon lords, whispered in the ears of kings and queens."

We reached the study, and I lit the candles with a wave of my hand. Lizbeth stood at the doorway, her legs swinging idly.

"But you want to know what it was like before I came here, don't you?" she asked, her eyes meeting mine.

I nodded, settling into my chair. "If you're willing to share."

Lizbeth's lips curved into a small smile. "I was... restless. Bored, even. When you've lived as long as I have, it's easy to fall into a routine. The same games, the same tricks, over and over again."

She walked over to me unfurling her wings and reverting slowly to her demon form. "I was looking for something new, something exciting. And then..." She gestured around the room. "Here I am."

I frowned, sensing there was more to the story. "But why were you drawn to my summoning? Surely you've resisted such calls before."

Lizbeth's eyes glittered in the candlelight. "Ah, now that's the interesting part, isn't it? Your spell was... different. Powerful in a way I hadn't encountered before. It intrigued me." She said while moving closer to me. "You intrigued me, Aaron Kelley. A mortal with such potential, such raw talent. How could I resist?"

I felt my heart rate quicken as she approached. There was something predatory in her gaze, a hunger that had nothing to do with food.

"Lizbeth," I said, my voice low. "What are you doing?"

She smiled, revealing her fangs. "What does it look like, little warlock? It's feeding time."

With her hand reaching out, her fingers traced the line of my jaw. I shivered at her touch, feeling desire coursing through me.

"Don't worry," Lizbeth whispered, her lips inching towards mine. "I won't take much... But I think you'll find that you're willing to give quite a lot."

I knew I should insist on maintaining our boundaries. But as her other hand came to rest on my chest, I found myself leaning into her touch.

"Lizbeth," I breathed, my resolve crumbling as she smiled, triumphant.

Chapter 10:
Mutually Beneficial

LIZBETH

I could feel Aaron's heart pounding under my touch, his breath hitching as I moved closer. The energy of his desire was intoxicating, a heady mix of fear and anticipation that made my own pulse quicken.

He was so deliciously human, so fragile yet so strong. This tantalizing combination was one that I found myself craving more and more.

I pulled back slightly, giving him a chance to change his mind. But instead of pulling away, he reached up, his hand coming to rest on my cheek. His fingers were warm, a stark contrast to the temperature of my own skin.

With a soft growl, I leaned in, my lips capturing his in a searing kiss. His gasp was music to my ears, his taste like ambrosia. I could feel his energy, his life force, pulsing under my skin, a beacon in the darkness.

As we kissed, I could feel the energy flowing between us, a give and take ritual I relished in. It was a dance, a negotiation, a battle of wills. And as I took his energy, I could feel my own power growing, filling me up. But I wanted more.

I felt the heat of his gaze upon me, a tangible force that seemed to sear through me. The air around us grew thick with arousal. Aaron's eyes, dark and intense, locked onto mine, and for a moment, the world seemed to stand still.

His lips found mine in a desperate, hungry kiss, full of need and longing. It was a kiss that spoke of power and surrender, of a man who was used to being in control but had found himself willingly giving it up to the whims of a creature like me. I reveled in the taste of him, the intoxicating blend of sweetness and something darker, something wild.

As his hands explored my body, I could feel the crest that marked me as his familiar burning against my skin. It was a symbol of our connection, a testament to the magic that bound us together. And when his lips moved from mine, trailing a path of fire down my neck and chest, I felt the crest glow, a beacon of our shared power. With a thought, my clothes were off.

I could feel the roars of thunder roaming through me as Aaron's mouth closed around my breast, his tongue teasing the sensitive flesh. The sensation was exquisite, a pleasure that left me aching for more. With a low growl, I reached for him, my fingers making quick work of the buttons on his shirt. The fabric parted easily under my touch, revealing his lean, muscular chest beneath.

I pushed him back against the wall behind his desk, my body pressing against his as I claimed his mouth in another searing kiss. My hands roamed over his chest, tracing the lines of his tattoos, the symbols of his power. I could feel the beat of his heart under my palm, the rhythm matching my own.

As I kissed my way down his neck, I could feel the energy pulsing between us. I dropped to my knees before him, my hands deftly undoing his belt and pants, my eyes never leaving his.

The sight of him, hard and ready, enhanced my excitement. I took him in my hand, my fingers wrapping around his length, feeling the warmth of his skin. And then I took him into my mouth, my tongue swirling around the tip, tasting the saltiness of his arousal.

Aaron's hands found their way to my hair, his fingers tangling in the long, dark strands. He held me in place, his hips moving in rhythm with my mouth, his breath coming in ragged gasps. I could feel the power building within him, the energy that was uniquely his, and I knew that he was close.

With a final thrust, Aaron found his release, his body shaking with the force of it. I held him tightly, my hands on his hips, my mouth working to draw every last drop from him. The energy that flowed into me was electric, a rush of power that filled me with warmth and vitality.

As the last of his shudders subsided, I released him, wiping my mouth with the back of my hand. I could feel the crest on my breast cool, the glow fading as our connection settled into a new equilibrium. Aaron slumped against the wall, his eyes closed, a look of blissful exhaustion on his face.

I stood, my body humming with the energy I had taken from him. But I did not take more than we had agreed upon. I could sense the fatigue lurking beneath his post-climactic languor, a reminder of the day's exertions and the energy we had expended during our trip to the village's market. I decided to not drain him further, a sense of concern for him plaguing my mind.

I leaned in, pressing a gentle kiss to his lips. "Rest, my little warlock," I said, my voice soft and full of promise. "We have more days ahead of us, more nights like this to come." I said while smirking.

With a final, lingering glance, I stepped back, giving him the space he needed to recover. As I moved away, I could feel his energy coursing through my veins, a potent mix of his life force and mine intertwined. It was a pleasurable sensation, one that I feel I'd never grow tired of.

Aaron watched me through half-lidded eyes. Despite the exhaustion that clung to him, there was a spark in his gaze, a hunger that had not been fully sated. It was a look that promised more.

"Good night, Aaron." I said as sweetly as I could, walking towards the doorway.

"Good night...Lizbeth."

I opened the door to my room, the stone trinket from the vendor clutched tightly in my hand. I placed it on the small table by the bed, a symbol of the day's events. As I sat down on the edge of the bed, I couldn't help but think about Aaron.

He was an enigma, a puzzle that I couldn't quite figure out. He was powerful that much was clear, but there was something else about him that intrigued me. Something that drew me to him in a way that I couldn't explain.

I leaned back against the pillows, my eyes drifting closed as I pondered about the little warlock. I could still feel the energy that had flowed between us during our encounter. The power that had surged through my veins as I took his life force. It was a delicious sensation, one that left me feeling both satisfied and hungry for more.

But there was more to it than that. There was a connection between us, a bond that went beyond the physical. I could sense it every time I looked into his eyes, every time I touched him. It was a connection that I couldn't quite put my finger on, but one that I knew was there.

I sighed, my thoughts swirling like a storm in my mind. I didn't know what it was that I felt for Aaron, but I knew that it was something more than just desire. There was a part of me that wanted to protect him, to keep him safe from harm. And yet, there was another part of me that wanted to use him, to exploit his power for my own gain.

I shook my head and closed my eyes, letting the darkness envelop me. As I let sleep claim me, I dreamt of fire and shadow, of power and desire. I saw myself standing atop a tower, my wings spread wide as I surveyed the world below. And beside me, there was Aaron, his eyes glowing with an intensity that made my heart race. But there was a darkness lurking, a threat that I couldn't quite see. I could feel it closing in around us, a malevolent force that threatened to tear us apart. It was too late. The darkness had already taken hold, and I could feel myself being pulled away from him, my screams echoing through the night as I was swallowed up by the shadows.

I woke suddenly, my heart pounding in my chest as I tried to shake off the remnants of the dream. It was just a dream, I told myself, just a figment of my imagination. But as I looked around the room, I couldn't shake the feeling that there was something more to it.

Chapter 11: One Step Closer

AARON

As the door clicked shut behind Lizbeth, the sound echoed through my study. I stood motionless, my breath caught in my throat. The lingering scent of Lizbeth's unique fragrance seemed to mock my attempts at composure.

I could still feel the ghost of her touch on my skin, each point of contact a spark threatening to ignite a fire of desire. The phantom pressure of her lips against me was a primal response that no amount of magical training could suppress. The pull to her was getting ridiculously stronger. I felt it could consume me if I weren't careful; with her, I had to hold back—or at least try to. But I was a warlock, and control was my domain—or so I desperately told myself, even as I felt that control slipping through my fingers like sand.

With a herculean effort, I wrenched my gaze away from the door, fixed my clothes, and forced my thoughts to focus on anything except Lizbeth. I needed a distraction, something to ground me in reality and remind me of the precarious situation I was in.

Just then, I noticed the cat emerging from under my desk. I couldn't remember seeing it before, but my mind had been so preoccupied with Lizbeth that it was entirely possible I had simply overlooked it. The feline gazed up at me with its unblinking eyes, a picture of feline innocence that seemed almost comical in contrast to what we had just done.

"Hey there, stray," I murmured, bending down to scratch behind its ears. The cat purred, pressing its body against my leg. Was it always in here? Had it watched that exchange between Lizbeth and me? It was unnerving to think that I might have had an audience, even if it was just a cat.

But then again, I reminded myself that cats were often associated with magic and the supernatural. Perhaps there was more to this seemingly innocent creature than met the eye. I shook my head, dismissing the thought as paranoid. I couldn't afford to let my imagination run wild.

With a final pat on the cat's head, I headed towards the area where the portal had manifested. I needed to get back to figuring this out. After Lizbeth and I had worked on the spell last, I had left the study in disarray, papers and books everywhere.

My eyes scanned the debris of our magical endeavor, searching for... something. I wasn't sure what exactly, but I knew it when I saw it. Half-buried under a pile of ancient scrolls, a fragment of parchment caught my attention. The symbols etched upon its surface were like nothing I had ever seen, yet they called to something deep within me, a mystic understanding that bypassed rational thought and spoke directly to my magical core.

I reached for the fragment. The moment my fingers brushed against its rough edges, visions exploded in my mind.

I saw worlds beyond imagination, new realms, and beings that shook me as my mind reeled at the sight of them.

Gasping, I clutched the parchment to my chest, my heart pounding a frantic rhythm against my ribcage. This was no ordinary text—it was a key, a piece of the cosmic puzzle that could unlock the secrets of inter-dimensional travel. With shaking steps, I made my way to my desk, spreading out the fragment under the soft, pulsating glow of my study's lanterns.

The symbols danced before my eyes, their meaning tantalizingly close yet frustratingly out of reach. Deciphering these markings could be the key to mastering portal magic, to bending the very fabric of reality.

I reached for my grimoire from out of my desk, the leather-bound tome that had been my constant companion through years of magical study. Its pages held the sum of my knowledge, the record of my triumphs and failures, the roadmap of my journey into the unknown. Now, it would bear witness to perhaps my greatest discovery yet.

As I dipped my quill into the inkwell, a drop of midnight-blue ink fell onto the page, blossoming like a dark star. I began to write, my hand moving across the parchment with a will of its own. The words flowed from me in a torrent, a stream of consciousness that seemed to bypass my rational mind and come directly from some deeper well of understanding.

I transcribed the mysterious symbols from the fragment, my quill recreating their curves and angles with uncanny precision. Alongside them, I detailed the visions that had accompanied their discovery, struggling to capture in mere words the vast, mind-bending concepts I had glimpsed. I wrote of the energy that had coursed through the room during our experiment, attempting to quantify the unquantifiable to bring order to the chaos of raw, unbridled magic.

As I wrote, I found myself describing not just the portal and its effects but also the feeling of connection I had experienced. It wasn't just a connection to other worlds but to Lizbeth as well. At that moment when reality itself had bent to our combined will, I had felt a resonance between us, a harmony of purpose and power that transcended the physical.

The thought of Lizbeth sent a jolt through me, breaking my concentration for a moment. I realized that my body ached with a need that had nothing to do with magical exertion. The memory of her touch, the curve of her lips, and the glint in her amber eyes came rushing back, threatening to overwhelm me. I gritted my teeth, forcing myself to focus on the task at hand. There would be time to untangle the complex web of emotions later. For now, the pursuit of knowledge had to take precedence.

Hours slipped by unnoticed as I delved deeper into the mystery of portal magic. The world outside my study faded into insignificance, the rising and setting of the sun marked only by the changing quality of light that filtered through my tower windows. My quill scratched across page after page, filling them with theories and conjectures, with symbols and diagrams that charted a course toward the unknown.

As dawn approached once more, painting the sky in hues of lavender and gold, I finally set down my quill. My hand cramped from the hours of writing, and my eyes burned with fatigue, but a sense of profound satisfaction settled over me. I had taken a significant step forward in my quest for power and understanding, opening doors that I had never even known existed.

I closed my grimoire with a sense of reverence, running my fingers over its worn cover. Within these pages lay the potential to reshape the very nature of magic itself.

Rising from my desk, I stretched, feeling the fatigue of the night's efforts seep into my bones. My muscles protested, reminding me that for all my magical prowess, I was still bound by the limitations of my mortal form. I needed rest to allow my mind and body to process the monumental discoveries of the past hours.

As I made my way to my chambers, the grimoire clutched tightly against my chest like a talisman. My thoughts drifted once more to Lizbeth. What would she make of my discoveries? Could I trust her?

I collapsed onto my bed, the softness a stark contrast to the hard wooden chair I had occupied for hours. As sleep began to claim me, my mind conjured a final image: Lizbeth's amber eyes, swirling with the same cosmic energies I had glimpsed through the portal. In that liminal space between being awake and dreaming, I wondered if perhaps she was more than just a catalyst for my magical growth—perhaps she was the key to unlocking mysteries I had yet to even contemplate.

My last conscious thought before succumbing to exhaustion was a promise to myself—I would unravel the secrets of portal magic, push the boundaries of what was possible, and in doing so, perhaps finally understand the enigma that was Lizbeth.

Smiling a bit at the memory of Lizbeth's touch burning in my veins, I drifted off to sleep.

Chapter 12: Realization

AARON

The months following our accidental creation of the portal had passed in a blur of feverish research and cautious experimentation. Each day, Lizbeth and I pushed the boundaries of our combined magic. The tower, once my prison, had become a sanctuary of discovery.

I stood at my desk, poring over the grimoire that had become as much a part of me as my own shadow. The pages were filled with equations and quickly scribbled annotations, each representing a stride toward deciphering the mysteries of portal magic. My fingers glided over my elaborate designs, sensing the dormant energy thrumming beneath the ink.

"You're going to wear a hole in that page if you keep at it," Lizbeth's voice, tinged with amusement, broke through my concentration.

I looked up, blinking as my eyes adjusted from the close focus of my work to the wider room. Lizbeth stood in the doorway, a steaming mug in her hands and a soft smile on her lips. The sight of her still caught me off guard sometimes.

"I brought you some tea," she said, crossing the room with a grace that belied her otherworldly nature. "Thought you might need a break from... whatever you're doing over there."

Our fingers brushed as she handed me the mug, and I felt that familiar jolt of energy. "Thanks," I mumbled, taking a sip to hide the flush I could feel creeping up my neck.

Lizbeth leaned against the desk, her tail swaying gently behind her. "So, any grand breakthroughs? Or are you just admiring your own handwriting?"

I chuckled, shaking my head. "Actually, I think I might be onto something. Look here." I gestured for her to come closer, pointing to a complex series of symbols I'd drawn. "See how these lines intersect? I think that's the key to stabilizing the portal."

As I explained my theory, I could feel my excitement building. The pieces were falling into place, a puzzle I'd been working on for what felt like lifetimes finally taking shape. Lizbeth listened intently.

"Aaron," she said softly when I paused for breath. "Are you saying what I think you're saying?"

I nodded, a grin spreading across my face. "I think I've cracked it. I'm close to figuring out how to send you home."

The words hung in the air between us, heavy with implication. It wasn't until I saw the flicker of emotion cross Lizbeth's face—joy quickly chased by something that looked unsettlingly like fear—that the full weight of what I'd said hit me.

Home. I could send her home.

The realization crashed over me like a wave of ice water. All this time, I'd been so focused on solving the puzzle, on proving

I could master this impossible magic, that I hadn't stopped to consider what success would really mean.

"That's... that's wonderful news," Lizbeth said, her voice neutral. "You've worked so hard on this."

I swallowed hard, trying to recapture the excitement I'd felt just moments ago. "Yeah, it's... it's quite the breakthrough. I mean, there's still work to be done, but the basic principle is sound. I think."

Lizbeth nodded, her eyes darting around the room, looking anywhere but at me. "Of course. There's always more work to be done, isn't there?" She laughed, but it sounded forced. "Well, I should let you get back to it. Wouldn't want to interrupt the great wizard in his moment of triumph."

Before I could respond, she was gone, the whisper of her wings the only trace of her passing. I stared at the empty doorway, my tea cooling forgotten in my hands.

What had I done? I'd been so caught up in the thrill of discovery, in the pure intellectual challenge of it all, that I'd forgotten the most important thing. Lizbeth wasn't just some magical puzzle to be solved. She was... she was Lizbeth. Infuriating, fascinating, impossible, Lizbeth.

And I was working on a way to send her away. Forever.

I slumped into my chair, suddenly exhausted. The cat I still hadn't named jumped onto my lap, purring contentedly. I stroked its fur absently, my mind a mess of conflicting thoughts and emotions.

"What am I doing, cat?" I murmured. "I should be thrilled. This is what I've been working towards, isn't it? Mastering impossible magic, proving myself to... to who? My family? The magical community that exiled me?"

Unsurprisingly, the cat offered no answers. It simply curled up tighter, a warm weight on my lap.

As the night deepened, I sat there, staring at the grimoire that held the key to Lizbeth's departure. In that moment, surrounded by the fruits of my labor, I had never felt more lost.

Somewhere in the tower, I heard the soft sound of Lizbeth's voice. She sang a melody I didn't recognize but that tugged at something deep in my chest. It was beautiful and sad and somehow ancient, like a lament for something not yet lost.

I closed the grimoire with a soft thud and made a decision. Tomorrow, I will talk to Lizbeth. Really talk to her about everything we'd been avoiding these past weeks. About what this magic meant, about what we meant to each other.

But for now, I let the sound of her voice wash over me, a bittersweet lullaby in the quiet of the night.

Sleep eluded me that night, my mind a tumultuous storm of thoughts and emotions. When dawn finally broke, I felt as though I hadn't rested at all. I dragged myself out of bed, my limbs heavy with more than just physical exhaustion.

As I made my way to the kitchen, I caught sight of Lizbeth. She was perched on the windowsill gazing out at the awakening world. The morning light caught her profile, and for a moment, she looked more ethereal than ever.

"Good morning," I said, my voice rough with sleep.

Lizbeth turned, a small smile gracing her lips. "Good morning, Aaron. Did you get any rest?"

I shook my head, moving to put the kettle on. "Not really. Too much on my mind, I suppose."

"I see," she replied, her tone carefully neutral. "Well, I'm sure you have a lot of work to do today. Don't let me keep you."

Again with obvious avoidance, she slipped past me and out of the kitchen before I could respond, leaving behind only the faintest trace of her scent, sweet like flowers. I stared at the empty doorway, the weight of everything unsaid hanging heavy in the air.

As I waited for the water to boil, my eyes fell on a small crystal vial sitting on the counter. It was one of Lizbeth's creations, a potion she'd concocted to help me focus during long study nights. The sight of it catapulted me into a series of memories.

I remembered the day she'd first offered it to me, her eyes glinting with mischief as she'd dared me to try it. "Come on, little warlock," she'd teased. "Afraid of a little hellish brew from little old me?"

I'd taken it of course. My pride wouldn't allow otherwise. The rush of clarity that had followed was unlike anything I'd ever experienced. It was as if a veil had been lifted from my eyes, allowing me to see the patterns of magic with unprecedented clarity.

That memory led to another—the night we'd spent huddled over my grimoire, piecing together the fragments of the ancient text. Lizbeth's tail had swayed in concentration, occasionally brushing against my leg. Each time it did, a surge of energy would run through me that had nothing to do with magic.

The whistle of the kettle jarred me back to the present. I poured the water mechanically, my mind still lost in its recollection.

How had we gone from reluctant cohabitants to... whatever we were now? The change had been so gradual, I'd barely noticed it happening. Until now, when the prospect of losing her made everything painfully clear.

I wandered into my study, cradling the steaming mug of tea. The familiar sight of books and magical apparatus brought little comfort today. Instead, my eyes were drawn to the small changes Lizbeth had made in the space—a cushion here, a vase of flowers there—little touches that had transformed my austere workspace into something warmer, more alive.

Unbidden, an image flashed in my mind—the study empty of these touches returned to its former sterile state. The thought sent a sharp and unexpected pang through my chest.

"What am I doing?" I muttered, slumping into my chair.

I should be thrilled. I'm on the verge of a magical breakthrough that could redefine our understanding of travel. I've always wanted this, discovering and learning new things about our world.

When had she become so essential? When had her presence shifted from an inconvenience to what feels like a necessity?

I closed my eyes, remembering the first time we'd successfully merged our magics. The rush of power had been intoxicating, yes, but more than that, I remembered the look of wonder on Lizbeth's face. For a moment, all her careful barriers had dropped, and I'd seen something raw and beautiful in her expression.

"What is this feeling that's troubling me," I whispered. I sat there contemplating this feeling and after a moment my body went rigid. The realization hitting me with the force of a lightning bolt.

I let out a shaky laugh, running a hand through my hair.

"Am I developing feelings for a demon," I said, louder this time. "A being from another realm, who I accidentally summoned and have been trying to send home. Brilliant, Aaron. Really stellar work."

But even as I mocked myself, I felt a sense of clarity settling over me. The conflict that had been tearing me apart suddenly seemed simple. Yes, I had made a breakthrough in portal magic. Yes, I could potentially send Lizbeth home. But did I want to?

More importantly, did she want to go?

I stood up abruptly. It was time to talk to Lizbeth. No more dancing around the subject, no more hiding behind magical theory and polite distance.

I strode towards the door, purpose in every step. As I reached for the handle, I heard Lizbeth's voice drifting from the other side. She seemed to be talking to someone, her tone urgent and low.

I froze, my hand hovering inches from the door. Who could she be talking to? We were alone in the tower, isolated from the rest of the world.

Curiosity and a twinge of something that might have been jealousy warred within me. Before I could decide whether to announce my presence or listen further, I heard something that made my blood run cold.

"I can't stay here much longer," Lizbeth was saying. "It's time for me to go home, with or without his help."

The words cut through me. All my newfound resolve crumbled in an instant, replaced by a sickening sense of loss.

I stumbled back from the door, my mind reeling. Had I misread everything? Had I been fooling myself all along?

As the implications of what I'd overheard washed over me, one thing became crystal clear: I had to find a way to keep Lizbeth here, to make her want to stay. And I had to do it soon, before it was too late.

Chapter 13:
Conflicted

LIZBETH

When Aaron stumbled into the kitchen, looking as though he'd aged years overnight, it took every ounce of my self-control not to reach out to him. Instead, I played the part of the nonchalant houseguest, exchanging pleasantries before making my escape.

Once alone, I looked around at the room I was beginning to call my own. I had given it my own touch a few weeks ago. I do quite like the crafts they have in this realm. There are many things to purchase to add flare to a space. Everything is so different here. Every time I am in the mortal realm, there seem to be endless things to see. I looked through my window at the sun, painting the sky in hues I'd never seen in the infernal realms. Even after all this time, this world's beauty still caught me off guard. It was so different from my home's harsh, unforgiving landscape—softer, more alive. Like Aaron.

The thought of him sent a familiar ache through my chest. I'd heard him tossing and turning all night, no doubt grappling with the implications of his magical breakthrough. Part of me wanted to go to him, to offer comfort or distraction. But I held back, unsure of my place in his world.

I let out a shaky breath. "Pull yourself together, Lizbeth," I muttered, pacing the confines of my room. "You're a demon, for chaos' sake. You don't get attached to mortals."

Somewhere along the way, between heated arguments and late-night study sessions, between accidental touches and shared laughter, I had done the unthinkable. I've become too familiar with this human.

I caught sight of myself in the mirror and barely recognized the being staring back at me. My wings were folded tight against my back, and my tail curled protectively around my legs. I looked... vulnerable. It was not a look I was accustomed to.

"What am I doing here?" I asked my reflection. "This isn't me. I'm Lizbeth, scourge of a thousand realms, temptress extraordinaire. I don't pine after awkward warlocks with beautiful eyes and a heart too big for their own good."

But even as I tried to summon my old bravado, memories flooded my mind. The way Aaron's face lit up when he solved a particularly tricky magical equation. The gentleness in his touch when he tended to my wing after a spell gone wrong. The sound of his laughter, rare and precious, filling the tower with warmth.

I slumped onto my bed, burying my face in my hands. "I can't stay here much longer," I said, my voice muffled. "It's time for me to go home, with or without his help."

The words tasted like ash in my mouth. Home. What did that even mean anymore? The infernal realms held nothing for me now, no challenges, no joys, nothing but endless monotony. But could I truly call this tower, this realm, home?

More importantly, could I call Aaron home?

I stood abruptly, my wings flaring out in agitation. "This is ridiculous. I'm a demon, not some sentimental mortal. I don't need anyone or anything."

But even as I said it, I knew it wasn't true. I needed the thrill of discovery that came with exploring this new magic. I needed the comfort of quiet evenings spent reading by the fire, Aaron's cat purring contentedly in my lap. I needed...

"I need him," I whispered. The admission was terrifying but also liberating.

But did he need me? Want me? Or was I just a fascinating magical puzzle to be solved and then discarded?

The memory of Aaron's excitement as he announced his breakthrough flashed through my mind. He had been so caught up in the magic, in the potential for travel, that he hadn't seemed to realize what it would mean for us. For me.

I thought to myself for a moment. If he's so eager to send me home, perhaps that's exactly what I should do. Leave before I get in any deeper. Before I lose myself completely.

But the thought of leaving, of never seeing Aaron again, sent a pain through me so sharp it was almost physical. I pressed a hand to my chest, surprised by the intensity of the feeling.

"Is this what it means to be human?" I wondered aloud. "To feel so much it hurts?"

I moved to the window, looking out at Aaron's world—a world of sunrises and gentle rains, books and tea, and quiet moments of connection. I wasn't sure I could leave it behind, and I don't know if someone like me belongs in it.

"I have to talk to him," I decided. No more games, no more hiding behind sarcasm and seduction. I need to know if there's a place for me here. With him." In all my centuries of existence, I had never made myself so vulnerable.

Composing myself to seek him out, I heard a knock coming from the entrance doors of the Tower.

Visitors? Here? In all our time together, Aaron and I had been wonderfully, terrifyingly alone. I wasn't sure if I was ready for that to change. I thought as I began transforming into my human form.

I heard Aaron's footsteps hurrying down the stairs and found myself following, curiosity overriding my earlier resolve to have a heart-to-heart talk. As I descended, I schooled my features into a mask of casual indifference. I couldn't let Aaron see how much his presence affected me, not yet.

We met on the lower floor, Aaron's eyes widening slightly as he saw me. "Lizbeth," he said, his voice catching a little. "I... there's someone at the door."

"I heard," I replied, arching an eyebrow. "Expecting company, were we?"

Aaron shook his head. "No, I have no idea who it could be."

As we approached the door together, I could feel the tension radiating off him. It occurred to me that these might be the first visitors he'd had in a while. I fought the urge to reach out and comfort him. Instead, I focused on maintaining my aloof demeanor.

Aaron took a deep breath and opened the door. On the other side stood two young humans. A man with an easy smile and a woman whose beauty rivaled that of most humans I'd encountered. I felt an immediate, irrational surge of dislike.

"Aaron!" the man exclaimed, pulling him into a hug. "Gods, it's good to see you!"

"Richard? Sophia?" Aaron stammered, clearly shocked. "What are you doing here?"

The woman—Sophia, stepped forward, her green eyes scanning the room before settling on me. "We came to check on you, of course," she said, her voice warm but with an undercurrent I couldn't quite place. "It's been too long."

I watched as Aaron's face cycled through a range of emotions —surprise, joy, anxiety. "I... it's wonderful to see you both," he said finally, stepping back to allow them entry. "Please, come in."

As they entered, Aaron seemed to remember my presence. "Oh, um, this is Lizbeth," he said, gesturing vaguely in my direction. "She's my... housemaid."

Housemaid? I barely managed to keep the incredulity off my face. Is that what we were going with?

"Charmed," I purred, letting just a hint of my true nature color my voice. I saw Sophia's eyes narrow slightly, and I had to suppress a smirk. So, she wasn't as oblivious as she appeared.

"Lizbeth," Aaron said, a note of warning in his tone that only I would recognize, "would you mind preparing some tea for our guests?"

I inclined my head, the perfect picture of a dutiful servant. "Of course, master," I replied, unable to resist the small jab. I saw Aaron wince slightly and counted it as a small victory.

As I moved towards the kitchen, I heard Sophia's voice drift after me. "So, Aaron, a housemaid? That's... new."

I lingered in the doorway, just out of sight, enhancing my hearing allowing me to eavesdrop effortlessly.

"Ah, yes," Aaron replied, sounding flustered. "It's a recent arrangement. The tower was getting a bit... unmanageable on my own."

Richard laughed. "Well, it certainly looks better than the last time we were here. Though I have to say, she doesn't exactly look like any housemaid I've ever seen."

If only you knew, I thought, a wry smile tugging at my lips.

"So, Aaron," Sophia's voice again, soft and intimate in a way that made me twitch with irritation. "How have you been? Really?"

I could practically feel Aaron's discomfort from here. "I've been... managing," he said after a pause. "My research has been progressing well. Actually, I've made a bit of a breakthrough recently."

"That's wonderful!" Sophia exclaimed, and I had to give her credit— she sounded genuinely pleased for him. "I always knew you'd do great things, Aaron. Even when... well, you know."

The silence that followed was heavy with unspoken history. I found myself gripping the tea tray so hard I could break it. Who was this woman to Aaron? What place did she hold in his heart?

Taking a deep breath, I composed myself and stepped back into the room, tea tray balanced perfectly in my hands. "Your tea," I announced, setting it down on the low table.

"Thank you, Lizbeth," Aaron said, his eyes meeting mine for a brief moment. I saw a flicker of... something there. Apology? Regret? Before I could decipher it, he looked away.

As I poured the tea with practiced grace, I observed the dynamics at play. Richard, relaxed and jovial, clearly an old friend. Sophia, beautiful and poised, her eyes rarely leaving Aaron's face. And Aaron, caught between joy at seeing his friends and obvious discomfort at the situation.

"Will there be anything else?" I asked, my tone perfectly respectful even as I met Sophia's gaze with a challenge she couldn't quite understand.

"No, thank you," Aaron replied. "That will be all for now."

I nodded and turned to leave, feeling Sophia's eyes boring into my back. As I reached the doorway, I heard Richard's voice, low and teasing.

"So, Aaron, are you going to tell us the real story about your 'housemaid,' or do we have to guess?"

I smirked to myself as I watched on from the stairs, wondering how Aaron would talk his way out of this one.

Chapter 14:
Unexpected
Reunions

AARON

I forced a laugh, trying to ignore the knowing looks Richard and Sophia were exchanging. "Very funny, Richard. Lizbeth is exactly what I said, a housemaid. Nothing more, nothing less." The lie felt heavy on my tongue, but I pressed on. "Now, are you going to tell me what really brought you all the way out here? I doubt it was just to critique my hiring practices."

Sophia leaned forward, her green eyes pinning me with concern. "Well, we were hoping you might be able to help us with something, actually."

"Oh?" I raised an eyebrow, curiosity piqued despite myself. "And what might that be?"

Richard cleared his throat. "There's been some... strange occurrences back in the capital. Magical disturbances that no one can explain."

I felt my heart rate quicken. Could they be referring to the aftereffects of my portal experiments? I kept my face carefully neutral. "What kind of disturbances?"

"They're calling it a 'magic quake,'" Sophia explained, her voice lowered as if sharing a secret. "Sudden surges of magical energy that seem to come out of nowhere. It's causing quite a stir."

"And you thought I might know something about it?" I asked, unable to keep a hint of bitterness from my voice. "I'm touched that you still think of me as a valuable source of knowledge, given my current circumstances."

Sophia reached out, placing her hand on mine. The gesture, once so familiar, now felt strange. "Aaron, you know we never agreed with your exile. We've always believed in you."

I gently withdrew my hand, noticing Lizbeth watching the interaction from the corner of the staircase. Her expression was unreadable, but I could sense a tension in her posture.

"Well, I'm afraid I can't help you," I said, standing up abruptly. "I've been here, isolated from the magical community, remember? Whatever's happening in the capital, I assure you I have nothing to do with it."

Richard stood as well, his expression concerned. "We know that, Aaron. We're not here to accuse you of anything. We just thought... well, you've always had a knack for unconventional magic. We hoped you might have some insights."

I softened slightly at his words. "I appreciate the thought, truly. But I'm afraid I'm as in the dark as you are."

Sophia bit her lip, a gesture I remembered all too well from our days at the university. "We're actually here without permission," she admitted. "We can only stay a night or two at most before we have to head back."

"I see," I said, feeling a mixture of relief and disappointment. "Well, you're welcome to stay, of course. It's... it's good to see you both."

The rest of the day passed in a blur of catching up, shared memories, and carefully avoided topics. I found myself constantly aware of Lizbeth's presence, hovering at the edges of our conversations. Every time I caught her eye, I saw a glimpse of something dangerous there, a reminder that our own unresolved tension was simmering just beneath the surface.

As night fell, I showed Richard and Sophia to their rooms, grateful for the tower's many spare chambers. I was heading back to my own room when a familiar voice stopped me in my tracks.

"Well, well, little warlock. Quite the reunion, wasn't it?"

I turned to find Lizbeth leaning against the wall, her amber eyes glowing in the dim light of the hallway. She pushed off the wall and sauntered towards me, her movements liquid and predatory.

"Lizbeth," I said, my mouth suddenly dry. "I was just about to turn in for the night."

She clicked her tongue, shaking her head. "Now, now. Surely you haven't forgotten our... arrangement? It's been quite some time since you've seen to my needs." Her voice dropped to a sexy whisper. "Or have your old friends made you forget all about little old me?"

I swallowed hard, feeling heat rise to my cheeks. "Lizbeth, I... this isn't the time. With Richard and Sophia here—"

"Oh?" she purred, now close enough that I could feel the heat radiating from her body. "And when will be the right time, Aaron? When your friends leave? When you finally figure out how to send me home?" Her eyes flashed dangerously. "Or perhaps you're hoping your pretty little Sophia might rekindle an old flame?"

"That's not—I didn't—" I stammered, thrown off balance by her sudden intensity.

Lizbeth placed a finger on my lips, silencing me. "Shh, don't worry. I'm not asking for much. Just a reminder that I'm here.

I stood there, frozen in indecision. Part of me wanted to give in, to lose myself in the intoxicating presence of this beautiful being who had become so central to my life. Another part recoiled, aware of the complications, the dangers, the unresolved feelings between us.

As Lizbeth leaned in, her lips barely a breath away from mine, I couldn't fight it anymore my resolve crumbled.

I gave in... It was a moment of weakness, of surrender. But I knew I made the right decision as soon as Lizbeth's lips met mine. The kiss ignited a fire within me that threatened to consume me. I was lost in her, drowning in the intoxicating taste of her kisses, the sweetness of her lips, the warmth of her breath.

We stumbled into my room, the door slamming shut behind us, sealing us from the outside world. As our lips parted, I couldn't help but reach for her again, my hands finding the smooth fabric of her dress. I wanted to feel her skin, to explore every inch of her body with my fingers and my lips.

I gently pulled at the neckline of her dress, revealing a hint of her delicate collarbone and the swell of her breasts.

My fingers traced the line of the fabric, slowly sliding it off her shoulders and letting it pool at her feet. She stood there before me, hiding nothing—her shamelessness begged to be punished. I paused momentarily, taking in her perfect skin, flushed with desire.

Her skin was a canvas I wanted to trace with my fingers and my mouth. I ran my hands up her arms, feeling the softness of her skin and the slight tremble of her muscles. I brought my lips to her neck, placing soft kisses along the delicate skin, tasting her with my tongue.

My hands moved to the curves of her breast, taking note of the fullness. Cupping them in my hands, my thumbs brushing over her nipples, causing her to gasp and arch into me.

I wanted to take my time to explore every inch of her, but the burning desire between us was too intense. I made quick work of my clothes using magic— I didn't want to waste a single second. My hands found her waist, and slowly, I lowered her down onto my bed, my body covering hers as our skin finally pressed together. I could feel her heart pounding against my chest, her breath hot on my cheek as I kissed her deeply.

Then, with a sudden flare, Lizbeth took control, her hands roaming over my body with a possessiveness that resonated within me. She was a creature of passion and desire, and she was claiming me as her own. I responded in kind, my hands exploring her body, learning every curve, every dip, every secret she had to offer.

Her skin was soft, like silk under my fingers, her body endlessly inviting. My fingers traced lines over her skin, leaving a trail of goosebumps in their wake. I could feel her tremble under my touch, her breath hitching in her throat as my fingers ran up her thigh and to her entrance. She was drenched in slick, and I pushed a little further, the sensation maddening. I worked my fingers inside her as she writhed beneath me, letting out the sweetest sounds.

With my free hand, I cupped one of her breasts and lowered my mouth over her nipple, rolling it between my lips, feeling it harden under my tongue. She gasped, her back arching off the bed, her hands tangling in my hair. I could feel her desire, her need, and it fueled my own.

I moved down her body, my lips trailing a path down her stomach, my hands spreading her thighs wide. I looked down at her, my eyes meeting hers, and I saw a blaze in her gaze, the hunger. I knew she was as ready as I was, and I couldn't wait any longer.

I buried my face in her, my tongue licking at her, tasting her, devouring her. She was sweet and tangy, and I couldn't get enough. I felt her hands in my hair, guiding me, urging me on. I could feel her body tense, her breath coming in short, sharp gasps. " Aaron," she gasped, pulling my face towards her lips. I kissed her, allowing her to taste herself on my lips.

I positioned myself between her legs. Looking into her glowing eyes, I knew this was more than physical desire. Without another thought, she pulled me close with her legs, her body begging for me to be inside her. Pre-cum dripping slowly from my tip, it was hard to resist.

Leaning forward my eyes never leaving hers, she wrapped her arms around my neck. and pulled me in for another kiss.

I fought with my desire to thrust my cock right inside her at that very moment. It was all too much how she clung to me—the temptation was staggering. Rubbing the head of my cock on her clit, I already had to squeeze the base of my cock hard, trying not to cum embarrassingly fast, and then I eased into her. Hearing her voice and mine gasping in unison at the sensation.

Being inside her was overwhelming, and I struggled to maintain my composure. My body ached for release, but I forced myself to go slow, savoring every moment. Each time I thrust into her, Lizbeth responded with equal intensity, her hips rising to meet mine in a perfect rhythm.

Our bodies moved together as if we were one. I leaned down to kiss her neck, my lips tracing a path along her collarbone. She let out a soft moan, her fingers digging into my back.

As we moved together, I felt a sense of euphoria wash over me. It was more than just physical pleasure, more than just the thrill of being with someone who made me feel alive.

But even as I savored the moment, I knew that it couldn't last forever. I could feel the pressure building inside me, the urge to let go and give in to the overwhelming sensation. And I knew that Lizbeth could feel it too, the way her body tensed and quivered beneath mine.

For a moment, I hesitated. I didn't want it to end, didn't want to break the spell that had been cast between us. But then she looked up at me, her eyes filled with a fierce intensity that took my breath away.

"Don't hold back," she whispered, her voice barely audible above the sound of our bodies moving together. "I want all of you."

And with those words, I let go. I gave myself over to the moment as we climaxed together. I felt a sense of release that was unlike anything I had ever experienced before.

For a moment, it was as if time itself had stopped. The world around us faded away, leaving only the two of us and the intense connection that bound us together.

But then, slowly, reality began to seep back in. I could feel the sweat dripping down my forehead, the way my heart was pounding in my chest. I looked down at Lizbeth and saw the satisfied smile that played across her lips.

"Well," she said, her voice low and husky. "Same time tomorrow?"

I couldn't help but laugh, the sound ringing out in the quiet of the room. It was a strange feeling, to be able to laugh and joke after something so intense. But somehow, it felt right.

Slick with sweat and our hearts pounding, we nestled into each other my arms wrapped tightly around her. She fell asleep almost instantly and I felt a sense of contentment that I hadn't felt in a long time.

And as I finally drifted off to sleep, I couldn't help the ache I felt in my chest, knowing this moment was limited and Lizbeth... She may soon decide to leave me here—to leave, me.

Chapter 15:
Breakfast and
Bedlam

LIZBETH

I stirred awake before the first light of dawn, my senses attuned to the subtle shift in the air signaling the approaching day. For a moment, I lay still, savoring the warmth of the bed and the lingering scent of our nocturnal activities. Today, I was determined to play my part to perfection. Housemaid extraordinaire, at your service.

However, I couldn't help but smile as I recalled the events of last night. Aaron had finally given in to his desire for me, and the experience was unlike anything I had ever encountered before. It was more than just physical gratification; there was an emotional connection that I hadn't expected.

I remembered the way Aaron had looked at me, his eyes filled with lust and adoration. He had been more vigorous than usual, his passion fueled by his newfound willingness to accept our connection. The sex had been both romantic and sensual, a side of myself I hadn't known existed.

My body craved the intimacy we had shared, but I resisted the urge to wake Aaron. Instead, I allowed myself to indulge in the fantasy of our night together, each detail etched into my mind.

My thoughts drifted to Sophia, and I couldn't help but feel a twinge of jealousy. She had a connection with Aaron that I couldn't compete with, and it irked me. But I pushed those feelings aside, focusing instead on the pleasure I had experienced with Aaron.

I reveled in the knowledge that I had claimed him over Sophia, if only for a single night. The power dynamic had shifted, and I found myself relishing in her loss.

As the sun began to rise, I slipped out of bed, careful not to disturb Aaron's slumber. Still in my human form from yesterday, I waved a hand and was now in my 'housemaid' attire. Then, I made my way to the kitchen. Smirking at the absurdity of it all. Here I was, Lizbeth, scourge of a thousand realms, about to prepare breakfast like some common mortal. If my fellow demons could see me now, they'd die of laughter. Probably literally.

I set about gathering ingredients, eggs cracked with a flick of my wrist, bread toasted with a subtle burst of hellfire. It was almost too easy, really.

Lost in thought, I almost didn't notice Sophia's entrance. Almost.

"Oh," she said, her voice dripping with false sweetness. "You're up early."

I turned, plastering on my best servile smile. "Good morning, Miss Sophia. I hope you slept well?"

Her eyes narrowed slightly, scanning me from head to toe. I felt a flicker of irritation. If she was looking for horns or a tail, she'd be sorely disappointed. I was the picture-perfect mortal.

"Quite well, thank you," she replied, moving further into the kitchen. "I thought I might help with breakfast."

"That's very kind," I said, returning to my task. "But unnecessary. It's my job, after all."

Sophia hummed noncommittally, leaning against the counter. "So, Lizbeth. That's an unusual name. Where are you from, exactly?"

And so it begins. I suppressed a sigh, keeping my tone light. "Oh, you know. Here and there. I've traveled quite a bit."

"Is that so?" Sophia pressed. "And how did you come to work for Aaron? He's never mentioned hiring help before."

I shrugged, focusing on plating the food. "It was a chance encounter. The right place at the right time, I suppose."

"Hmm," Sophia mused, her tone sharpening. "Speaking of encounters, I couldn't help but notice some... unusual noises last night. Coming from Aaron's room."

I froze for a split second, fighting to keep my composure. A thousand retorts danced on the tip of my tongue, each more scathing than the last. But I swallowed them down, along with the urge to show this presumptuous mortal exactly who she was dealing with.

Instead, I turned to her with wide, innocent eyes. "Oh my. I do hope the tower isn't haunted. Perhaps we should perform an exorcism?"

Sophia's cheeks flushed, her eyes flashing with barely concealed jealousy. "That won't be necessary. I'm sure there's a perfectly reasonable explanation."

"Of course," I agreed smoothly, secretly reveling in her discomfort. But beneath my satisfaction, a tendril of concern unfurled. How much had she heard? How much did she suspect?

Before Sophia could continue her interrogation, Aaron and Richard entered the dining area. I breathed an internal sigh of relief, gathering up the breakfast trays.

"Good morning, everyone," I chirped, the perfect picture of a dutiful servant. "Breakfast is served."

Aaron and I shared a knowing look. His cheeks bloomed with a delightful shade, and I felt a surge of satisfaction course through me. I couldn't help but smile at his expression.

I moved around the table, distributing food and pouring tea, but I started to question if I would fit in here. I couldn't help but feel like an outsider looking in. Aaron, Sophia, and Richard fell into easy conversation, peppered with inside jokes and shared memories. I hovered at the edges, refilling cups and pretending not to listen.

"So, Aaron," Sophia said during a lull, her voice deceptively casual. "Have you given any thought to returning to the capital? I'm sure if you just spoke to the council—"

"There's nothing to discuss," Aaron cut her off, his tone sharper than I'd ever heard it. "They made their decision. I've made mine."

An awkward silence fell. I busied myself by clearing empty plates and stealing looks at the strained scene.

Aaron's jaw was clenched, his eyes fixed on his cup. Sophia looked frustrated, while Richard seemed oblivious to the undercurrents, happily munching on his toast.

"Well," Sophia said finally, "At least you're not completely alone out here. You have... Lizbeth... to keep you company."

The way she said my name made my tail twitch beneath my glamour. I turned, ready to deliver a cutting remark disguised as innocent small talk, when a thunderous bang echoed through the tower.

Instinct took over. I dropped the plates I was holding, spinning to face the threat. My wings itched to unfurl, my claws longed to extend. Protect Aaron. The thought blazed through my mind with surprising intensity.

But before I could act, a figure burst into the room. He was tall, dark-haired, with features strikingly similar to Aaron's. But where Aaron's eyes held warmth and curiosity, this man's burned with an almost manic intensity.

"Jed?" Aaron gasped, rising to his feet. "What in the hell are you doing here?"

"Where is she?" Jed demanded, his gaze sweeping the room before landing on Sophia. "Ah, there you are, my dear. Do you have any idea how worried I've been?"

Sophia had gone pale, her earlier confidence evaporating. "Jed, I can explain—"

"Oh, I'm sure you can," Jed cut her off. "Just like you can explain why you're here with my brother instead of preparing for our wedding."

Wedding? My eyes darted between Sophia and Jed, then to Aaron, whose face had gone slack with shock.

As chaos erupted around me—Aaron demanding explanations, Sophia trying to placate both brothers, Richard attempting to play peacemaker—I took a moment to assess the situation. This new arrival complicated things enormously, but it also presented opportunities. After all, chaos was my natural element, but somehow, I felt off about this whole situation.

Chapter 16: Family Ties Unraveled

AARON

The world seemed to tilt on its axis as I stared at the figure in the doorway. Jed, my brother, was here, in my sanctuary, his presence jarring. The air in the room was suddenly heavy, charged with an electric tension that made the hairs on the back of my neck stand up.

"Jed?" I managed to choke out, my voice barely above a whisper. "What in the hell are you doing here?"

A flood of emotions crashed over me—surprise, anger, and, beneath it all, a traitorous hint of longing. For a moment, I was transported back to our childhood, before rivalry and bitterness had poisoned everything between us. Memories flashed through my mind—Jed and I, barely more than toddlers, chasing each other through the sprawling gardens of our family estate. The pride in his eyes when I first manifested my magical abilities. The gradual shift as that pride turned to envy, then to contempt.

But Jed's eyes, so like my own yet burning with an intensity I'd never possessed, snapped me back to reality. His gaze swept the room, landing on Sophia with laser-like focus. I felt my stomach clench, sensing the storm that was about to break.

"Ah, there you are, my dear," he said, his voice dangerously soft. "Do you have any idea how worried I've been?"

The words were gentle, but the underlying threat was unmistakable. I'd heard that tone before, usually right before Jed unleashed his temper. My body tensed instinctively, ready to intervene if necessary.

Sophia had gone pale, her earlier confidence evaporating like morning mist. "Jed, I can explain—"

"Oh, I'm sure you can," Jed cut her off, his tone dripping with sarcasm. "Just like you can explain why you're here, with my brother, instead of preparing for our wedding."

Wedding? The word hit me like a physical blow. I looked between Sophia and Jed, my mind reeling. Sophia, engaged? To my brother? When had this happened? And why hadn't she told me? The betrayal stung, sharp and unexpected. I'd thought Sophia was here out of concern for me, maybe even... but no. Once again, I was just a pawn in someone else's game.

"What's going on?" I demanded, my confusion quickly giving way to frustration. "Sophia, what is he talking about? Jed, why are you here?"

Sophia's eyes darted between Jed and me, her lips moving, but no sound came out. She looked like a cornered animal, desperate for escape. Jed, for his part, kept his gaze fixed on her as if the rest of us didn't exist. The intensity of his stare was unsettling, borderline possessive.

"I... I'm sorry, Aaron," Sophia finally managed. "I should have told you. Jed and I... we're engaged. It was arranged by our families, to unite our houses. I came here to... to..."

She trailed off, unable or unwilling to finish the sentence. But Jed had no such reservations.

"To what?" Jed snapped. "To run away? To rekindle an old flame with my exile of a brother?"

The accusation hung in the air, heavy and suffocating. I felt a surge of indignation, both at the implication and at being kept in the dark about something so significant.

"I had no idea about any of this," I shot back. "Sophia and Richard showed up yesterday, out of the blue. If I'd known she was engaged—to you of all people, I would have sent her right back."

Even as I said the words, I wasn't sure if they were entirely true. Would I have turned Sophia away? Or would I have selfishly clung to this unexpected connection to my old life, regardless of the consequences?

From the corner of my eye, I noticed Lizbeth shifting slightly, positioning herself between Jed and me. The gesture sent a confusing mix of emotions through me—appreciation for her protection, fear of her secret being exposed, and something else—something warm and unfamiliar that made my heart race.

Richard, ever the peacemaker, stepped forward. His face was a mask of calm, but I could see the tension in the set of his shoulders, the way his hands were slightly raised, ready to cast a spell if needed.

"Look, there's clearly been a misunderstanding here," he said, his voice steady and reasonable. "Why don't we all calm down and talk about this rationally?"

I felt a rush of gratitude for my friend's level-headedness, even as worry for his safety gnawed at me. Jed had never been known for his rational thinking, especially when his pride was at stake. And right now, his pride had taken a serious blow.

"Stay out of this," Jed snarled at Richard before turning his anger towards me. "And you. I should have known you'd be behind this. Couldn't stand the thought of me having something you didn't, could you?"

His words stung more than I cared to admit. They dredged up old insecurities, reminding me of all the times I'd felt second-best, the black sheep of the family. But beneath the hurt, anger began to simmer. How dare he come to my home and accuse me of such things?

"You're delusional," I spat back. "I didn't even know you two were engaged. I've been here, exiled, remember? The exile you so enthusiastically supported."

I saw a flicker of something—guilt? Or was it regret that crossed Jed's face, but it was instantly replaced by a sneer.

"Oh yes, your exile," he said, his voice dripping with contempt. "Tell me, brother, have you enjoyed your time away? Cultivating your 'unconventional' magic? Corrupting others with your influence?"

I felt something snap inside me. Years of pent-up anger and hurt came rushing to the surface.

"Corrupting? That's rich, coming from you," I snarled. "At least I have the courage to pursue what I believe in, instead of blindly following family tradition like a good little puppet."

The moment the words left my mouth, I knew I'd gone too far. The tension in the room became thick with the promise of violence. I could feel the magic building, responding to our heightened emotions. It was like standing in the eye of a storm, knowing that at any moment, chaos would erupt.

Jed's hands clenched at his sides, and I saw the telltale flicker of flames dancing at his fingertips. His control was slipping, and with it, any chance of resolving this peacefully.

Time seemed to slow down. I was acutely aware of everyone in the room Sophia's wide-eyed fear, Richard's tense posture, Lizbeth's coiled readiness. And Jed, my brother, his face twisted with rage and hurt.

In that moment, I had to make a choice. Protect my friends and expose my secrets, or maintain the facade I'd built and risk everything. The decision weighed heavily on me, each option loaded with potential consequences.

As Jed's control finally snapped, flames erupting from his hands, I made my decision. Whatever came next, I knew nothing would ever be the same.

"Enough!" I roared, throwing up my hands. Dark energy crackled between my fingers, forming a shimmering barrier between Jed and the rest of us. The flames from his hands splashed against it, dissipating harmlessly.

Jed's eyes widened in shock, then narrowed in fury. "So it's true," he spat. "You've been dabbling in the dark arts. Have you no shame, Aaron? No respect for our family's legacy?"

I laughed bitterly. "Legacy? You mean the legacy that cast me out for daring to question the status quo? The legacy that values obedience over innovation?"

As we argued, I was acutely aware of the others in the room. Sophia had pressed herself against the wall, her face a mask of horror. Richard stood protectively in front of her, his own hands glowing with defensive magic. And Lizbeth... Lizbeth had moved to stand beside me, aiming to get my attention.

"Aaron," Lizbeth said softly, her eyes meeting mine as she turned to address me. Her expression held concern. Before I could respond, a blinding flash erupted at the edge of my vision, illuminating the side of her face. My heart lurched as I realized what was happening. It was Jed, he had simultaneously launched an attack of great magnitude towards us. The energy of his spell filled the air. There was little I could do to react in that split second, my mind racing to process the sudden turn of events.

Chapter 17: Bonds Shattered

AARON

The room exploded into chaos. One moment, I was staring into Jed's rage-filled eyes; the next, a wall of fire was rushing towards me. I barely had time to push Lizbeth out of the way and throw up my arms in a futile attempt at protection before the blast hit me.

The impact was staggering. I felt myself flying backward, crashing through the tower wall that I had always believed to be impenetrable. Stone and mortar crumbled around me as I tumbled into the open air, the ground rushing up to meet me.

Pain lanced through my body as I hit the earth, the breath knocked from my lungs. As I gasped for air, blood running down my face, the reality of what had just happened sank in. Jed, my own brother, had actually tried to kill me.

Before I could fully process this, I saw Richard leap from the gaping hole in the tower, his face set in grim determination. He landed beside me, hands already moving in the intricate patterns of earth magic.

"Stay behind me, Aaron," Richard grunted, raising a stone wall between us and the tower.

Jed's laughter, cold and mocking, rang out. "Hiding behind your friends, brother? How typical." Another fireball slammed into Richard's barrier, causing cracks to spiderweb across its surface.

I struggled to my feet, my body protesting every movement. "Jed, stop this madness!" I shouted. "We don't have to fight!"

"Oh, but we do," Jed snarled, launching another attack. This one shattered Richard's wall, sending chunks of rock flying. "It's time you learned your place, Aaron. Time you understood what real magic is!"

As Richard hastily erected another barrier, I began weaving my own spell, reinforcing his defenses with a layer of energy. It wasn't much, but it was all I could manage in my battered state.

"Real magic?" I retorted, anger giving strength to my words. "Is this what you call real magic? Attacking your own brother?"

Jed's response was another barrage of fireballs, each one more intense than the last. Richard and I struggled to maintain our defenses, the heat becoming unbearable.

"Jed, please!" Sophia's voice cut through the roar of flames. She stood at the edge of the destroyed wall, her face pale with fear. "This isn't you! Stop before someone gets seriously hurt!"

For a moment, Jed hesitated, his eyes flickering to Sophia. But then his face hardened once more. "Stay out of this, Sophia. This is between me and my dear brother."

"Richard," Jed called out, his voice deceptively calm, "I have no quarrel with you. Step aside, and let me teach Aaron the lesson he so desperately needs."

Richard stood his ground, sweat pouring down his face from the effort of maintaining his spell. "Not a chance, Jed. I won't let you hurt him."

Jed's eyes narrowed. "So be it."

The air around Jed began to shimmer with heat. I could feel the magical energy building, far stronger than anything he'd unleashed so far. With a sinking heart, I realized that our combined defenses may not be enough to stop what was coming.

"Is this what you wanted, Aaron?" Jed shouted, flames dancing around his entire body now. "To see what I'm truly capable of? Well, brother, prepare to witness true magical prowess!"

As Jed gathered his power for a final, devastating attack, time seemed to slow. I saw Sophia screaming, her words lost in the roar of the flames. I saw Richard, steadfast and determined, pouring every ounce of his strength into our defense. And I saw Jed, my twin, his face twisted with anger.

Limited on time, I was forced to make a choice. With the resolve to no longer hold back, I didn't think, didn't hesitate, I simply reacted. With a gesture, I tore open the fabric of space just as Jed's attack breached Richard's barrier. The meteor-shaped ball of impending death disappeared into the vortex, revealing my new original spell to all present. The shock on all their faces was unmistakable.

For a moment, stunned silence reigned. Then, a blur of movement caught my eye. Lizbeth, moving faster than I'd ever seen her, launched herself at Jed. But it wasn't Lizbeth in her human form, she had dawned horns and her tail, with her body cloaked in a powerful miasma. A creature of nightmares and dark beauty, wings unfurled, tail lashing, eyes blazing with deadly fire.

Before I could cry out, she struck. Jed went flying, a strangled scream escaping his lips as Lizbeth's claws raked across his chest. He hit the ground hard, blood staining his torn shirt.

"No!" The word tore from my throat before I could stop it. Despite everything, he was still my brother.

As silence fell over the battlefield, Jed lay sprawled on the ground, his chest heaving. The sight of him lying there, injured and vulnerable, sent a shock of horror through me.

I turned to Richard and Sophia, dreading what I'd see in their eyes. Richard's face showed disbelief, his mouth opening and closing without sound. Sophia had both hands clamped over her mouth, her eyes wide with terror.

"Aaron," Richard finally managed. "What... what just happened? Who—what is Lizbeth, really?"

I felt a surge of defensiveness at the fear in his tone.

"Original magic and sh... she's Lizbeth,"

But even as I said it, I felt off about something was it disappointment? or shock? I couldn't tell. Seeing her viciousness on full display, I couldn't help but feel a flicker of the same fear I saw in my friends' eyes.

"Original magic?" Sophia's voice was high-pitched, bordering on hysterical. "Lizbeth?... Aaron, don't you see, she's a demon!"

Hearing Sophia's outburst, I looked at Lizbeth with my eyes wide from the intensity of the situation. Unable to find the right words to respond, my thoughts jumbled.

Lizbeth turned to face me, her eyes meeting mine. In them, I saw a swirl of emotions—confusion, hurt, and betrayal. Not only did I fail to claim her as my familiar, as someone who meant... something to me, but in my act of surviving my brother's attack, I had also revealed the secret I'd been keeping from her.

"Lizbeth, I—" I began, but she cut me off.

"Save it," she snarled, her voice echoing with power. "I should have known better than to trust a mortal like you."

Her words stung, igniting a spark of anger within me. "Trust? How could I trust you when half the time I never know what's real when I'm with you?"

"Real?" Lizbeth laughed, a bitter, hollow sound. "That's rich, coming from you. Tell me, Aaron, when were you planning to mention that you've finished the *portal* spell? That you could have sent me home at any time!?"

I felt the blood drain from my face. But even as my answer formed, I knew it didn't matter. The hurt in her eyes and voice was all too much.

"I was going to tell you," I said weakly, knowing how pathetic it sounded even as the words left my mouth.

"When, Aaron?" Lizbeth demanded. "After you'd finished using me for your experiments? After you'd learned all you could from me?"

Each accusation felt like a slap in the face. I wanted to deny it and explain that it wasn't like that, but the words wouldn't come. Deep down, a part of me wondered if she was right.

But how could I tell her that I wanted her to stay when she seemed so readily willing to leave?

As we argued, I became aware of a building pressure mounting in my chest. The magic that bound us, the connection we'd forged over these past months, was straining under the weight of our unstable emotions.

"Lizbeth, please," I said, reaching out to her. "Let's talk about this. We can—"

But it was too late. Lizbeth extended her wings and with a gust of wind, she took off. The backlash sent me staggering. I could only watch as Lizbeth flew to the top of the tower, entering through one of the windows. The feeling left me hollow and empty in a way I'd never experienced before.

For a moment, I stood there, frozen in shock. Then, the reality of the situation came crashing back. Jed was still bleeding on the ground. Richard and Sophia stared at me with a mixture of fear and confusion.

Sophia pulled herself from the shock of the situation and hurried over to my brother performing a healing spell on his wound. Fearing the worst, I rushed over there as well.

Jed groaned, stirring to push himself up as Sophia's magic slowly restored him back to consciousness.

"Jed, what were you thinking? I can't believe you'd put everyone here in danger like that." Sophia said. As she finished the healing spell she was casting.

"Me? Did you see that monster he's been harboring here at my uncle's tower? Look what she did to me." Jed replied.

"She's not a monster!" The vehemence in my own voice surprised me.

"Oh, spare us," Jed shot back, his voice raspy but still edged with bitterness. "Defending your pet demon now, brother? How touching."

"Can't wait to tell father about the twisted shit you've been up to out here. As if being exiled has taught you nothing. Does your shame know no bounds!" his words were as bitter as the blood he coughed.

Richard and Sophia looked at me expectantly, waiting for me to explain this entire situation.

"You don't understand," I said. "None of you do."

Richard stepped closer, his expression softening. "Then help us understand, Aaron. What's really going on between you and Lizbeth?"

I looked at him, seeing the genuine concern in his eyes. How could I explain something I was only just beginning to understand myself? The fear I felt seeing Lizbeth unhinged like that was daunting, but so was the ache in my chest at the thought of her leaving.

Before I could formulate a response, a tremor ran through the tower. We all looked up instinctively, and I felt my heart sink. Above us, the clouds were beginning to twist and churn, a vortex of magical energy growing larger by the second.

"Aaron," Richard said, his voice cutting through my daze. "What's happening?"

I looked up at the magical disturbance, my heart pounding as understanding dawned. "She's trying to leave," I said, the words feeling hollow.

The thought of Lizbeth leaving, of never seeing her again, sent a spike of panic through my chest. At that moment, all the confusion, fear, and doubt crystallized into a single, undeniable truth... I couldn't let her go.

"Go after her," Richard urged as if reading my thoughts. "We'll take care of things here."

I hesitated for a split second, torn between my responsibilities and my heart. Jed was injured, the tower was in shambles, and I owed my friends so many explanations. But the thought of losing Lizbeth forever...

With a nod of gratitude to Richard, I turned and raced into the tower. I took the stairs two at a time, calling Lizbeth's name. But as I burst into my study, I knew I was too late. The room was empty, except for the swirling vortex of energy hovering above my desk. A single feather, dark as night and smooth as silk, drifted through the portal, landing softly on the floor.

The crushing weight of loss settled over me. She was gone. And it was all my fault.

As I stood there, surrounded by the remnants of my shattered life, I made a silent vow. I would find a way to make this right. To bring Lizbeth back, to explain everything.

Whatever it took, I would find her. I had to. Because in losing her, I'd finally realized just how much she meant to me. And I wasn't ready to let that go.

Chapter 18: The Path of Vengeance

JED

Agony lanced through my body as I struggled to my feet, each movement a battle against the demon's lingering magic. The energy of it, I could feel, dissipating slowly around me. But it was my pride that bled most profusely, an invisible wound that cut deeper than the hit I had received.

Sophia's arm encircled my waist, her touch both comforting and galling. I couldn't tear my eyes away from the tower's gaping maw where Aaron had just disappeared, swallowed by shadows and secrets. The ancient stones seemed to mock me, whispering of failure and lost opportunities.

"Aaron!" I called out, my voice hoarse and raw, echoing uselessly against unyielding stone. But he was gone, chasing after that... creature. That abomination that wore beauty like a cloak, hiding poisonous intent beneath an alluring facade. A maelstrom of emotions churned within me; white-hot anger at being bested, the bitter bile of humiliation, and a twisting knife of betrayal knowing my twin had chosen a demon over his own blood.

Richard's steady and resolute voice cut through my tumultuous thoughts. "I'm staying," he announced, his jaw set in that familiar stubborn line I'd come to resent over the years.

"Aaron might need help."

A surge of resentment coursed through me, as potent as any spell. Of course, loyal Richard, always there for Aaron. It had been that way since we were children—Aaron, the golden boy, surrounded by devoted friends while I stood in the shadows, watching, waiting, burning with a desire for a recognition that never came.

"Fine," I spat out, unable to keep the venom from my voice. The word tasted like ash on my tongue. "Go. Chase after your precious Aaron and his pet demon. I'm sure he needs you far more than the magical authorities need to know about this breach of every law we hold sacred."

Richard gave me a long look, and I saw a kaleidoscope of emotions swirl in his eyes—pity, disappointment, and something else... understanding? For a moment, I felt exposed, as if he could see right through the walls I'd constructed. But he said nothing. He just turned and followed Aaron into the tower, swallowed by the same darkness that had claimed my brother.

Sophia gently tugged at my arm, her touch feather-light yet insistent. "We should go," she said softly, her voice a melody of concern and urgency. "You need medical attention, and we need to report this to the council. What we've seen here... it changes everything."

The council. Yes. The word ignited a spark in my mind, and I felt the first tendrils of a plan begin to take root, pushing aside the pain and humiliation. I nodded, allowing Sophia to support me as we began our journey back to the capital. Each step sent jolts of pain through my body, but I welcomed it. Pain was clarifying. Pain reminded me of what was at stake.

As we walked, I replayed the battle in my mind, each moment etched in vivid detail. The surge of Aaron's power, the tear in reality itself, the glimpse of impossible vistas beyond the portal's shimmering surface. My failure burned, but I couldn't deny the shock I felt at Aaron's display of power. Portal magic? When had he learned such a thing? And to what end? The questions stirred in my mind a tornado of possibilities and dangers.

"I can't believe it," Sophia said, breaking the silence that had settled between us like a shroud. Her voice trembled slightly. "A demon. Aaron was living with a demon all this time."

I seized the opportunity her words presented, like a drowning man grasping at a lifeline. "Who knows what else he's been hiding?" I said, carefully modulating my voice to strike the perfect balance between concern and righteous anger. "Portal magic, demon summoning... Aaron has always pushed the boundaries, but this? This is beyond reckless. It's a danger to the very essence of our world."

Sophia nodded, her brow furrowed with worry, and I saw my words taking root. Good. Let the seeds of doubt grow. Let them flourish into a forest of fear and suspicion.

The journey back to the capital took two days, each hour a crucible in which my plan was forged and refined. By the time the familiar skyline of home came into view—the towering spires of the Mage's Academy piercing the sky like accusatory fingers, the bustling magical marketplaces thrumming with arcane energy—my resolve was as hard as diamond.

In the privacy of my quarters, surrounded by the trappings of the life I'd built, I allowed myself a moment of doubt. The face that stared back at me from the ornate mirror was haggard, eyes sunken with exhaustion and something darker. Was I doing the right thing? Aaron was my brother, my twin, the other half of the whole we once were.

But then memories flooded back, as vivid and painful as the day they were formed. Every slight, real or imagined. Every moment I was passed over in his favor, my accomplishments diminished in the blinding light of his so-called genius. Every patronizing word of encouragement from our parents, their eyes always sliding past me to rest adoringly on Aaron. My reflection's expression hardened; doubt burned away in the trenches of resentment. Aaron had made his choice. Now he'd face the consequences.

I spent hours crafting my narrative for the council, each word chosen with the precision of a master alchemist measuring rare ingredients. I wove a tapestry of half-truths and methodically crafted lies designed to paint a picture of a rogue mage delving into forbidden magics, heedless of the risks to himself and others. In my tale, I was the reluctant hero, forced to stand against my own blood for the greater good.

As I stood before the council, resplendent in their robes of office, I could feel the weight of their gazes upon me. The chamber thrummed with tension and anticipation. I launched into my prepared speech, my voice resonating with practiced sincerity.

"Esteemed members of the council," I began, my tone grave, "it is with a heavy heart that I come before you today. What I have witnessed... what I must report... it shakes me to my very core."

I described Aaron's dangerous association with the demon, the mysterious and terrifying portal magic he wielded. With each word, I watched their reactions carefully, a maestro conducting an orchestra of emotions. Concern showed on their faces, fear widened their eyes, and outrage tightened their jaws. I had them in the palm of my hand, puppets dancing to the tune of my design.

"Members of the council," I concluded, allowing a tremor to enter my voice, "it pains me more than I can express to speak against my own brother. But I fear Aaron has strayed too far from the path of responsible magic use. He poses a threat not just to himself, but to the very foundations of our magical society. We must act, and act decisively, before it's too late."

As they deliberated, I maintained a mask of somber concern, all the while feeling a heavy mix of triumph and a small, quickly suppressed jerk of guilt. When they announced their decision—that Aaron was to be considered a threat and arrested immediately—I allowed myself a moment of visible struggle before nodding in reluctant agreement.

"I... I understand," I said, my voice thick with feigned emotion. "It pains me deeply, but I cannot deny the wisdom of your decision."

One of the council members, an elderly woman with silver hair, leaned forward. "Jed, we know this must be difficult for you. Are you certain you can handle what comes next?"

I straightened my shoulders, squaring them as if bearing a great burden. "I assure you, Madam Councilor, I am prepared to do whatever is necessary for the safety of our magical community. Aaron may be my brother, but our duty to protect others must come first."

"Well said, young Kelley," a gruff voice added from my left. "Your loyalty to our principles is commendable."

I inclined my head in acknowledgment, allowing a flicker of pain to cross my features. "Thank you, sir. I only hope that one day, Aaron will understand why this had to be done."

As the council members nodded in approval, I couldn't help but savor the sweetness of my victory. Aaron, my dear brother, your time in the spotlight was finally over. Now, it was my turn to shine.

Later, alone in the shadowed corners of the council chambers, I savored my victory. Though, for a brief moment, regret threatened to surface, a ghostly hand tugging at my conscience. But I pushed it down ruthlessly, fortifying myself with memories of every moment I had been in Aaron's shadow. This wasn't just revenge, I told myself. This was justice, long overdue.

As I began to plan my next moves, my keen ears caught whispers from a group of younger council members. They spoke of Aaron's magic not with the fear I had so carefully cultivated, but with poorly disguised intrigue. Words like "potential" and "valuable" reached me, and I realized that neutralizing Aaron might not be as simple as I had thought.

"Did you hear about the unconventional spell Aaron's been developing?" one of them murmured, excitement evident in his tone.

Another responded, "I know! It's fascinating. Imagine the applications if we could harness that kind of power."

Their enthusiasm grated on my nerves, threatening to unravel all my hard work. I clenched my fist, feeling the cool metal of my signet ring press against my skin. This wouldn't do at all. I needed to act fast, to redirect their curiosity before it gained momentum.

Plastering on my most charming smile, I sauntered over to the group. "Gentlemen," I said smoothly, "I couldn't help but overhear. You seem quite interested in my brother's... experiments."

They looked up, startled by my sudden appearance. I could see the moment they realized who I was, their eyes widening with a mixture of respect and wariness.

"Master Kelley," one of them stammered, "we were just discussing—"

I cut him off with a wave of my hand. "Oh, I'm well aware. But tell me, have you considered the risks involved? The potential for catastrophe?" I leaned in conspiratorially, lowering my voice. "After all, there's a reason such magic has never been done before."

As I spun my web of exaggerations, I could see doubt creeping into their eyes. Good. Let them remember why Aaron was exiled in the first place. I'd make sure his magic remained a threat, not an opportunity, in their minds.

The council's decision echoed in my mind, a vindication of everything I'd worked towards. Yet, as I stood before them, maintaining my mask of reluctant duty, a part of me marveled at how easily they had accepted my narrative. Years of resentment, of being overlooked, had honed my ability to manipulate situations to my advantage. I'd learned to wield words as deftly as any spell.

As I bowed and prepared to take my leave, a sudden thought struck me. This couldn't be the end of it. Simply setting the hounds on Aaron's trail wasn't enough. No, I needed to be there, to see this through to its bitter conclusion.

A new determination took hold, steel replacing the blood in my veins. I had to be the one to bring Aaron in. Not just to prove my superiority once and for all, but to ensure he didn't somehow turn this to his advantage. I'd lived in his shadow for too long, watched from the sidelines as he basked in adoration he never truly cared about. It was time to step into the light, to claim the recognition that should have been mine all along. Whatever the cost.

Preparing to retire for the night, my mind raced with plans and possibilities, a labyrinth of schemes and contingencies. Soon, the hunt would begin in earnest. And this time, I wouldn't let Aaron best me. This time, when the dust settled and the magic faded, I'd be the one left standing. And the magical world would finally see which Kelley twin truly deserved their respect, their admiration, their fear.

In the mirror, my reflection smiled back at me, a predator's grin full of anticipation. Let Aaron have his demon and his portals. I had ambition, intellect, and the full weight of magical law behind me. The game was afoot, dear brother. May the best twin win.

www.ingramcontent.com/pod-product-compliance
Lightning Source LLC
Chambersburg PA
CBHW071957150726
47999CB00001B/467